I0779151

The
DRUM TECH

and
Other Stories

MONTE CRABBS

RAVEN VIEW

To my wife, Lisa—without your encouragement,
these stories would have remained untold.

And to my sons, Daniel and Joseph—may your love of
reading continue to grow with every page you turn.

Contents

Echoes in the Halls

BILL OTTINGER, the high school principal, was working late in his office. He liked this time of day more than the rest. He found it funny that his chosen profession involved working with numerous children and teachers, yet he relished the times when neither were present.

He pressed the power button on his laptop computer and waited until the login screen appeared. It welcomed him to the Four Oaks Computer Network and prompted him to type in his username and password. Because it took about three minutes to fully initialize the system, he usually had time to browse other items on his desk and sneak a snack from his treat drawer. But today was different. Instead of opening to his familiar computer desktop scene—the one with a picture of his dog Max—the computer opened to a black screen with only three words at the top: *Who are you?*

"Now what?" Bill said aloud. *This must be some prank by one of our lovely students who is too smart and has too much time on their hands*, he thought. "I don't have time for this."

He sat there staring at the screen, his face turning bright red. His hand went immediately to the phone to press the extension to the library where Glenn Gorman worked as not only the school librarian but also the computer teacher and all-around tech guy. The call went instantly to Glenn's voicemail. Of course, it was late, and he was home with his family. Bill leaned forward and spoke into the phone with a very practiced, caring, and positive voice. "Mr. Gorman, please call me in the morning when you get this message. I think . . . no, I'm sure we're having another student computer hacking issue. I'll give you more details when you call. I'm sure you'll get to the bottom of this matter—you always do. Bye for now." He pressed the end-call button.

The computer hacking problems seemed never-ending. Mr. Gorman was trying to stay on top of the issues with his limited knowledge. Then Bill remembered a brochure he had received in the mail a few days earlier. He had thought it was strange and kept it out of curiosity. Now he considered it with a fresh perspective. Maybe it could help solve his problem.

He opened his top desk drawer to retrieve the flyer. It read:

Robot Investigator for Hire

The future is now. Do you have a mystery to solve? Have you tried other sources only to spend lots of money with no return? Time to think outside the box. AI is your friend. If you feel your organization plays on the cutting edge, then call us now. Operators are waiting, and they are all human—or are they?

The brochure also included a few pictures of ordinary people doing ordinary tasks. *They do look human,* he thought, *not like the robot servers that you saw more and more in restaurants.* And the testimonials on the back side of the brochure were all positive. However, they would never post negative reviews on their own materials.

On the inside was a list of benefits to having a robot investigator come into your company, pose as an employee, and work on solving mysteries with no one being the wiser. The one that caught his eye was item ten out of ten. It stated: Robots don't make mistakes. "Sold!" he said with a smile.

He looked back at the screen. Now, in addition to the previous question, the statement *I really want to know!* had been added, prompting an old Who song to pop into Bill's head. *Enjoy the joke while you can*, he thought. Then he typed, *Next time use a song from your own generation.* Smiling at his own sense of humor, he went to power off the computer. Then, another line printed out under his entry.

Maybe I did.

The screen flickered, and then there was Max looking at him with those constantly smiling eyes he adored.

What is normal? This is a question Rob Cooper had often asked himself.

As he looked in the mirror, his reflection showed all indications of normality. He was young—early twenties. His auburn-colored hair was moussed to perfection. His clothing was in style, from his red, collared shirt to his crisply ironed Dockers. All was in place.

He stepped closer to the mirror, examining his teeth. Yep, they were all there straight and vivid white.

A noise from the kitchen caught his attention, and he looked away from the mirror. The tea kettle was blasting away as the steam escaped. Rob removed the kettle from the burner just before the boiling water erupted.

Is drinking tea a normal way to start a day, he wondered? *Maybe I should have chosen coffee.* He had no intention of drinking either of them; he just wanted to fit in with the other teachers.

Today was a big day. He was being placed as a student teacher in the English department at Four Oaks High School, an experimental undertaking that had been in the works for decades. The project was considered top secret and details of the organization responsible and people involved were not readily available—not even to Rob. What he did know was that he was well educated in classroom instruction, and he was being placed under an English teacher named Mr. Johnson. Was Mr. Johnson aware of the project? Rob had no idea. If successful, this could mean the total replacement of human teachers. *Won't the teachers' unions be thrilled about that*, Rob thought, and chuckled.

He seemingly had memories of his past, starting from childhood, where he grew up in a mountain community, and continuing through his college years attending a highly respected teachers' university in northern Colorado. Rob thought this strange because his creation day was only three years ago. He was twenty-three years old, but in reality, he was only three. *There's one for the books*, he thought. The memories, as realistic as they were, could only be part of the programming. Yet these memories were extremely vivid. Almost too vivid. He considered this to be a flaw in the programming. A normal adult would have memories, but many of the details would fade over time. His did not. He could remember playing games with his brother, Dave; they were running from imaginary creatures only they could see. *When was the last time he had been with Dave?*

Rob knew he was not human in any sense of the definition. He was a robot, plain and simple.

He looked at his watch; it was 6:30 a.m.—time to get going. It was never a good idea to be late on your first day. Rob flipped his wrist over and slid his watch toward his hand about two inches. Grabbing a small tab, barely visible at first glance, he pulled gently, exposing a small computer screen within. One tap and the screen silently came to life. Various boxes appeared with pictures indicating their function. Rob pressed the box with a calendar picture and his schedule for the day came into view. It had been updated; not by him, but by his programmers. Rob scanned through the pages of dialogue and then closed the wrist panel. *This will be an exciting day,* he thought. The notes described this as his first day of interaction with the outside world, but how could that be? He had memories of many interactions. But he knew they were dummy memories— nothing that actually happened, just strings of code designed to give him the experiences necessary to cope in the real world of humans.

Rob walked to the kitchen sink and dumped out his untouched tea and headed toward the entryway of his small apartment. Now to gather the things he needed for the day. He was given a leather briefcase that held the necessary student teaching document, a few pens, and his lunch. Not much, but he didn't need much.

Rob walked down the hall to the front door, pausing a moment to look at himself one last time in the foyer mirror. Yes, indeed, he was a normal-looking guy. Rob smiled and left the house.

The drive to school was uneventful. His car was equipped with all the latest safety devices that, when he wrapped his fingers around the steering wheel, became networked into his central processor. Rob and the car were one functioning network.

He entered a large parking lot next to a sign that read *Four Oaks High School*. The high school was of an average size for Colorado, serving around 450 students in four grades. The socioeconomic status of the students varied from above-middle-class families to extremely poor, lower-class families who received benefits from the federal government. Apparently, this knowledge was being fed to him through his onboard computer network.

Rob pulled into an open parking spot, got out, and scanned the school's campus. The lot was about half full with a number of adults weaving in and out of the parked cars, heading toward the building. The teachers were greeting each other with handshakes and hugs—most had not seen each other for a couple of months. This was the first day of a new school year, the first of three days set aside for meetings and classroom preparation. Rob was to attend these meetings and help his supervising teacher, Mr. Johnson, in his classroom.

First, though, Rob was looking for someone else. Her name was Ms. Susan Moss, and she was his technical liaison from the Robot for Hire organization. To everyone else at the school, she was a professor from the University of Northern Colorado. From his programming, he knew Ms. Moss was an extremely attractive middle-aged woman and would be easy to identify. He quickly caught sight of her in the parking lot. Her medium-length brown hair was blowing across her face in waves as she glided across the asphalt. She moved with the grace of a cat despite the towering heels of her dress shoes. Was she also a robot?

"Hi, Ms. Moss," Rob shouted and waved his hand as he opened the back door of his car to grab his briefcase.

"Rob! Great to see you. We have a few items to go over before your meeting with Mr. Ottinger, the principal," she said without hesitation. She pulled out what looked like a normal flash drive from her purse and proceeded to lift his hair above his back collar and insert the drive into a well-concealed USB slot. "Nice to meet you too," he said as he looked about to see if this totally not-normal greeting had been observed by anyone else in the parking lot.

"Sorry," she said as she removed the drive and slid it silently into her purse. "Most of your programming is done remotely, but there was this one rather large item I needed to take care of. In the future, if needed, I'll be more discreet—I promise."

"No harm done. I'm sure to be the most inconspicuous teacher with a hole in the back of my head in the school." He winked at her, and they headed to the front door with everyone else.

The halls of the school were wide and sparsely populated by teachers, all going in separate directions. "Follow me," Ms. Moss said as she disappeared into an office with a large sign informing all guests to check in at the main office promptly.

Inside, a well-kept elderly woman looked up from her desk. "May I help you?" she asked. The placard on her desk was inscribed with *Hello, my name is Miss Olsteen* in shiny gold letters.

"My name is Susan Moss, and this is Rob Cooper, the new student teacher for Mr. Johnson. I believe that Mr. Ottinger is expecting us this morning."

"Yes, very good," Miss Olsteen said as she placed her coffee cup on a memo pad in the center of her rather large desk.

A balding man entered the office from the back and said, "Ms. Moss, how nice to finally meet in person. I'm Bill Ottinger. We spoke on the phone. Please come in and have a seat." His friendly smile was contagious, and Rob smiled back. The two followed Mr. Ottinger into his office.

The space was neatly fashioned except for the stacks of paper and notebooks that occupied every flat space available. The walls were covered with plaques announcing prestigious awards won throughout the years, along with Mr. Ottinger's academic diplomas, which were all neatly framed and strategically placed to show that this was a man who deserved to be in the position he held. Susan promptly shut the door once they were all inside. Immediately, the smile left Mr. Ottinger's face. What replaced it was a look so intense it sent a shiver down Rob's robotic spine.

"Will Mr. Johnson be joining us?" Ms. Moss asked.

"Not today. He's not to be informed about the nature of this project. Actually, all he knows is that he has been assigned a student teacher for the semester." Mr. Ottinger picked up a mug and took a long draw of coffee.

Coffee, Rob thought, *not tea. I'll stop and get a coffee pot on the way home.*

Mr. Ottinger, still scowling, placed his mug down and spoke in a soft but intense voice. "As you know, the success of this project relies on total discretion. Mr. Cooper here is a student teacher, and that's all anyone needs to know." He looked Rob in the eye with a harsh gaze that seemed a little threatening. "You have only been partially briefed as to your mission."

Mission seems a funny way to refer to a student teaching session, Rob thought.

"The rest will be revealed to you in small amounts during your time here at Four Oaks High School. At the present, let's just say that teaching the students literary composition and grammar will be a small priority. You should see the irony in that, or at least you will."

He pressed a button on his desk phone, and Miss Olsteen's friendly voice quickly answered. "Yes?"

Mr. Ottinger cleared his throat and once again spoke in his friendly voice. "Please inform Mr. Johnson that Mr. Cooper is on his way down. And would you be so kind as to give Mr. Cooper his name tag before he leaves the office? Thank you." He pressed the same button again to disconnect. Then the stern-faced Mr. Ottinger turned to Rob and said, "You'll be observing Mr. Johnson in action for the first couple of weeks." Then his eyes narrowed. "Stay alert, Mr. Cooper. This hacker, whomever he or she is, is tricky."

Ms. Moss and Rob walked out of the office together. Before they parted, she whispered, "When you get home, check the files that I downloaded into your port. This will give you all the details you need for this case. Having all the facts upfront will be to your advantage." Then with that, she left without another word.

That night, Rob accessed the case files.

The meetings were held in the school library, which contained several large tables, sturdy wooden chairs, bookshelves, and ten computer terminals. Rob was introduced to the rest of the teachers, who, in turn, introduced themselves and stated their teaching subject and number of years they had been teaching at Four Oaks High School. When it was Rob's turn, he stood up like everyone else had done and with a smile on his face said, "My name is Rob Cooper and I attend the University of Northern Colorado and will be student teaching in Mr. Johnson's classroom." Most of the teachers smiled back warmly. Rob learned that Mr. Johnson had taught for eight years and was excited to have his first student teacher.

The teacher meetings all took place in the morning, leaving the afternoon for working in the classroom. There was a lot to learn, and Rob was soaking it all up. The first afternoon was spent getting to know Mr. Johnson better and to learn the tasks of running a classroom, like operating the online student management system. He had not gotten a network login yet, so Mr. Johnson gave him his to use in the meantime. All clerical aspects of teaching were recorded and tracked with this software. Mr. Johnson learned that Rob was a fast learner, unaware that he had a computer system for a brain. "I think you and I will make a great team, Rob."

"Yes, I think we will." Rob smiled.

On Wednesday afternoon, the day before students arrived, Mr. Johnson encouraged Rob to explore the rest of the school. "I'll see you bright and early tomorrow." Mr. Johnson shook Rob's hand. "Don't fret too much about the first days. Your job will be to observe and to help when I need you. Also, never be afraid to help the students with any problems they might be having."

"Thank you," Rob said and walked out into the hall—he needed to find a computer.

There were many hallways and getting lost was a possibility. A couple of doors other than classrooms he passed were labeled "Boys" and "Girls." Restrooms, he figured. *I don't need them but should be seen going in one on occasion*, he thought. He opened the door to the boys' restroom and walked inside. The lights were off at first, but came on by themselves as he walked in further. "Nice touch," he said. *Always good to conserve energy.*

The room was large, with four closed stalls to one side and six urinals opposite them. They were only separated by a small partition that was bolted to the wall—*not much privacy here,* he thought. Rob turned to leave when one of the urinals behind him flushed all by itself. He turned, and immediately they all started flushing. He was a little confused by the concept of conserving electricity on one hand, then wasting water on the other. *The flushing systems must be faulty,* he thought as he opened the door to leave, then felt someone shove him out into the hall. Rob caught himself from falling and turned around to see absolutely no one behind him. He went back in to investigate and found no one in the restroom. Someone or something had pushed him, but whatever it was had vanished. Intrigued more than frightened, he stepped back into the hallway.

"Can I help you find something, Mr. Cooper?" asked a friendly voice from behind him.

Turning around, Rob found that the voice belonged to one of the teachers he had met in the morning meetings. She was the pretty business teacher named Kim Swenson. "Miss Swenson, yes, I think there's some kind of plumbing problem in the boys' room."

Miss Swenson immediately looked like she had just eaten sour milk. "I'll let Paula know. She's the head custodian."

Rob decided not to mention the force that had pushed him out of the boys' room.

"You remembered my name, impressive with everyone you just

met—but please call me Kim. I'm only Miss Swenson to the students, don't you know."

Rob remembered all that he heard, so he wondered, *Maybe I should pretend to not remember so that I'll appear more human.*

Remembering his original mission, Rob said, "Also, would there be a computer terminal that I could use?"

"There's one of the computer labs around the corner, or there's always the library."

He did need to visit Mr. Gorman in the library, but instead said, "The lab will be fine. Will it be okay to use one of the computers?"

"Of course. Did you get your login?"

"I'm sharing Mr. Johnson's for now."

Kim smiled and said, "I'm sure we could get Mr. Gorman, the librarian, to give you your own login, for Pete's sake."

"Yes, I need to do that." He followed her to the lab.

"Use any one you like—you can log in to any computer in the school. Just know that the internet is pretty locked down for security reasons."

"Thank you," he said as he turned to leave.

"You bet ja," she said in return. Rob loved her accent.

He sat down at one of the terminals at the back of the room, powered it on, and waited for the login page to load. He typed in Mr. Johnson's username and password and was eventually brought to Mr. Johnson's landing page with a variety of options. In the background was a serene mountain landscape. *I would love to visit a mountain someday*, he thought. Using a mouse device, he clicked on the button labeled Library Media Center and was taken to another page with more options. The button that caught his eye was labeled LOCAL HISTORY. "That might be a good place to start," he said aloud and clicked the button. Then, in the search box, he typed "Four Oaks High School" and filtered the search to only find newspaper articles.

The search resulted in hundreds of titles. *Perfect*, he thought, and began scanning the list. It took Rob about forty-five seconds to scan all 839 titles. Using a zip drive from his pocket, he downloaded some of the articles to read later. He still needed to find this Mr. Gorman in the library—he needed to get his own login, "for Pete's sake," as Kim had said—and he couldn't forget to stop for his coffee maker on the way home.

Mr. Glenn Gorman's name was on the entrance to the library. In addition to being the librarian, he was also the computer network technician and coach for all the boys' sports. *He was a busy man,* Rob thought, *which was probably why he was not at any of the in-service meetings.*

As Rob approached the library, an elderly lady hurried through the door in front of him. He followed her inside. She was already in the process of emptying the daily trash from under the circulation desk. "Um, excuse me," Rob said. "I'm looking for Mr. Gorman."

The woman looked up and seeing the suspicious look on her face, Rob continued, "Oh, I'm sorry . . . My name is Rob, Rob Cooper. I'm the new student teacher in Mr. Johnson's room."

"Hi. I'm Paula, the night custodian. Mr. Gorman is gone by this time every day. He's probably down in the boys' locker room getting ready for football practice. They have their first scrimmage this weekend, I hear. Him being gone is one of the reasons I start my duties here first every night."

"Makes sense to me," he said, wondering if Miss Swenson had had a chance to talk to her about the restroom problem.

"Do you want to know the other reason that I clean this room first?" she said.

"Ah, because the teachers are all in their rooms after school and Mr. Gorman has sports practice," he said.

"Yes, it's a little about that, but mostly I don't like being in here after dark. That's when the ghost talks to me, tells me to *go away*." She walked over to another trash basket, continuing her tasks. "He's always back there in that corner," she said, pointing to the back shelves under a sign that indicated it was the history section. "He sounds like an angry boy."

"Have you told anyone?"

"They don't listen."

"I'm listening—and I believe you," Rob said, wondering if there were any connections to the entity haunting the computer network and hacking into his own system or maybe the ghost in the boy's room.

"Well, thank you, but that's really all I know. I just avoid the library at night, not that I've ever felt totally threatened, but still, it's real creepy."

"Thanks, Paula, and it was nice to meet you. I'll just have to talk to Mr. Gorman tomorrow. Bye." Rob started to leave, then stopped to ask, "Did Miss Swenson tell you about the plumbing problem in the restroom down the hall?"

She looked confused at first, then smiled and said, "Oh, that's not a plumbing problem. We've already checked it out. I think our little ghost friend likes to flush toilets."

"Interesting," he said.

"Be safe, Mr. Cooper," she said as she went back to her work. "Seems like a nice young man," she added to no one in particular.

Rob walked back to the classroom, juggling the newfound clues.

After stopping at Walmart to purchase a coffeepot, Rob pulled his car into the parking lot of his apartment complex. *Tomorrow is the first day of school with students—how exciting,* he thought, as he parked and walked toward the stairwell. His apartment was on the second floor of a four-story building.

There were a few of his neighbors out and about, walking dogs, and acting normal. No one was paying the slightest bit of attention to him. Then again, why would they? He was about as normal as they came.

Carrying the new coffeepot under one arm, Rob dug in his pocket for his key. When he found it, he unlocked the door, made his way into the apartment, and headed straight to his MacBook Pro.

Why does a robot need a computer? Because all normal teachers have computers and know how to use them. Plus, it was easier for him to use than the tiny screen located in his left wrist—a feature he knew was being eliminated in the newer models. Rob could manage many of the functions of his MacBook using his built-in Bluetooth capabilities, but forced himself to always use the touch pad and the keyboard to navigate, on the outside chance someone was watching.

When the Mac was fully initialized and his password for entry was entered, Rob inserted his flash drive into the USB slot on the side of the computer. What he saw was totally unexpected. Along with the newspaper articles he had downloaded, the drive contained several

JPEG files. Double-clicking these files opened pictures of him at school that day—one was a picture of him sitting at the computer in the lab.

Someone is spying, he thought, *and they were able to put the files on my zip drive without me knowing. The fact remains, they also want me to know they are spying.*

Rob ejected the zip drive and filed it away into his desk drawer—he would deal with the articles later. He walked into the kitchen to set up his coffeepot. *Simple device, really*, he thought. *Not much to put together.* But after reading the directions, he realized they hadn't included filters or coffee grounds. *Oops*, he thought, and headed back to the grocery store.

In the morning, Rob made his coffee, poured it into a to-go cup, and headed to school excited about meeting the students.

Once in the building, Rob was mesmerized by the number of students who had invaded the hallways. Some gave him questioning looks, but most were more interested in talking to their friends. He saw Mr. Johnson standing by his door, waving for him to hurry.

"You're going to do fine—maybe get here a little earlier tomorrow," Mr. Johnson said.

"Oh, sorry, I was brewing my morning coffee that I enjoy drinking every day," he said. Mr. Johnson gave him a strange look—Rob noticed.

They walked into the classroom, and when the first bell rang, the students began filing in from the hallway.

As the students took their seats, Rob listened closely as Mr. Johnson started previewing the teaching unit for this semester, which was the reading and analysis of classic works by notable authors. The class was first studying the novel *The Old Man and the Sea* by Ernest Hemingway, reading the book outside of class and discussing the chapters in their time together. After they finished the novel, Mr. Johnson planned on showing the class a movie based on the book.

This novel was the shortest one on the class syllabus and was scheduled to be finished within two weeks. Rob had never actually read the book but knew everything there was to know because while listening to Mr. Johnson speak, he had downloaded the entire content along with all the analytical studies ever recorded. He was now an expert on not just *The Old Man and the Sea*, but all the works of Ernest Hemingway. From a few comments he contributed while Mr. Johnson was discussing the unit, Rob could tell that Mr. Johnson was extremely impressed.

"Mr. Cooper will be with us for the entire semester from the University of Northern Colorado," Mr. Johnson announced to the first-period class. "He's getting his degree in secondary education with an emphasis in language arts. Basically, he wants to teach English at the high school level, and this is his last step toward obtaining his goal. For a few weeks, he'll act as my helper—observing, grading papers, and assisting you on an individual basis. Then, eventually, I'll turn the class over to him." After a short rumble from the students, he continued with, "You'll be expected to treat him no differently than you treat me. Now, are there any questions for Mr. Cooper?"

"Are you married?" said a girl in the back of the room. This brought on some snickers from the class.

"No," said Rob, "but if you know of someone, let me know." The class erupted with laughter. "Actually," he continued, "I don't even have a girlfriend . . . or a boyfriend—much too busy with school now—my main focus will be all of you. It is truly an honor for me to be working with Mr. Johnson and to be allowed to hone my teaching skills. I'm looking forward to my time here, and I'm hoping I can teach you half of what I expect to learn from you. I'm excited to be able to try out some teaching methods that I have stored on my hard drive—I mean that I learned at the university. Sorry, my circuits, ah . . . my brain, that is, is in slight overload. Maybe I should reboot." The students were now staring at him. "Wow, don't know where that came from, I mean, I obviously don't have a hard drive." He laughed nervously. *Rats*, he thought to himself. *I look like a real teacher, therefore I need to talk like a real teacher.* It was obvious that he was making lots of mistakes with his first interaction with the students. *I'm not supposed to make mistakes*, he thought. He continued. "Let's just say it will be a pleasure working with all of you, and I'm sure we will get along splendidly." Rob looked over at Mr. Johnson for help.

Mr. Johnson quickly came to his rescue. "Thank you, Mr. Cooper. Now I need someone to help hand out the novels."

Introductions in the second and third period classes went more smoothly, so when Rob stood up in front of the fourth-hour class, he felt like a pro. Rob started talking about himself and adding way more than he had in the other periods.

He found he liked standing up and talking to people—he was a natural, or *maybe it is my programming*, he thought. He looked around the room at the students as he spoke and saw most were looking at him with some interest. One boy was picking at some-thing sticky on the bottom of his shoe. Another was yawning. *Was he being that boring?* Rob learned that it gave him more energy when he focused on the students who were not only paying attention but also smiling. He continued to scan the room. Then he noticed a slender, blond-haired girl near the back of the room. She looked terrified. Her mouth was hanging open in a way that looked like she was about to scream. She quickly brought her hand to her mouth to suppress what could have been a small gasp. *What a strange response*, he thought as he continued speaking. *I don't think my designers intended for me to be scary.*

After the introductions to the fourth-period class, Rob took his chair at the back of the room. On the way, he glanced over at the frightened-looking girl. She was still looking at him and moving her head back and forth slowly, as if in disbelief.

Mr. Johnson was passing out copies of *The Old Man and the Sea* to the students. "Please use the last ten minutes to read the prologue in the book," Mr. Johnson said. "Come tomorrow prepared to answer questions on the first three sections."

"Mr. Cooper, will you help me?" Rob looked up. The blonde girl was standing next to him. She was dressed in jeans, white Converse tennis shoes, and a black tee that read *I Have Issues* on the front in white lettering and *Korn* written on the sleeve.

I thought corn was spelled with a C, he thought, then said, "Of course I can help, what do you need?"

The terrifying look was back on her face. "It's not about school; it's about my brother. His name is Cory."

"Does he go to school here?"

"No," she said matter-of-factly. "He died."

Oh my, Rob thought. "I'm sorry to hear this," he said. "What can I do for you?"

"Cory told me to ask you for help. He called you by name." She paused shortly, looking like she didn't know what to say next. "And how could he know your name? I didn't even know you would be here."

"I thought you said he died." Rob was getting confused, and too much confusion could make his circuits overheat.

"Yes, I miss him so much," the girl replied.

Rob could feel the heat rising in his head. "Then how can he tell you to ask me for help?"

"I don't know, but he does." She smiled. "My name is Natalie."

"How can I help you, Natalie?" Rob was now dripping with what looked like sweat but was just water coming from his internal cooling system.

She seemed to notice and asked, "Are you okay, Mr. Cooper?"

"Yes, it's very hot in here," he said, trying to calm himself to keep his motherboard from frying. "How can I help?" he said again.

Natalie looked a little confused and rubbed her hands along her arms. She seemed to be nearly shivering. But she continued. "Can we talk after school? I'll meet you in the front benches while I wait for my bus."

"I'll be there."

As she took her seat, Rob was still contemplating the notion that live people can talk to dead people. After a few minutes listening to Mr. Johnson talk about Ernest Hemingway, his temperature was back down to an acceptable level.

After the school bell rang, indicating the end of the school day, Rob talked briefly with Mr. Johnson. "Sorry for my goofy start—just nerves, I guess."

"Already forgotten," said Mr. Johnson. "It will get better, I promise.

Now, don't feel like you have to hang around here. See you tomorrow." And he turned to the papers on his desk.

"See you tomorrow," Rob replied. He wanted to ask him about what Natalie had said, but Mr. Johnson was now busy doing whatever it is that teachers do, so he headed out to meet Natalie.

She was already waiting at the bench when Rob arrived. "I don't have much time," she said. "The buses are starting to line up."

"I think I must have misunderstood you this morning. You said your brother, Cory, told you something; something about asking me for help, yet you said he died?"

Natalie nodded her head.

"Did he die recently?" he asked.

"No—about four years ago—here at the school." Rob couldn't tell if she was about to cry or not. Then she continued dry-eyed. "He was the best big brother, so kind to everyone."

Rob's hard drive was spinning. *There was an actual death here at the school. Could Cory's spirit still be walking these halls and tormenting everyone? Could a person who was 'kind to everyone' become mean after death?* "I'm so sorry, Natalie. When did he talk to you?"

"This morning as I was waking up," she said, looking down at her feet. "It's like a dream, yet not a dream. I can't describe it." She looked at Rob. "Sometimes I can't remember what he says, but this morning, clear as I'm hearing you now, he said, 'Natalie, go to Mr. Cooper. Go to him and ask for help.' I asked him 'help for what,' but he was gone. So, I was kind of hoping you would know how you could help me."

"I can't think of any reason you need help. It can't be about schoolwork—we just started." The bus pulled up for the students to board. "I want to help, but in what way? I'm at a loss."

Natalie got up to get on the bus. She turned. "That's okay, Mr.

Cooper, maybe my brother will give more information sometime." She got on the bus and waved to him as it drove away. He waved back.

Now I have two mysteries to solve, he thought as he made his way to the teachers' parking lot.

Upon arriving back at his apartment, Rob quickly removed his laptop from his briefcase, powered it on, logged in, and inserted the flash drive into the USB slot. A list of PDF files appeared on the screen, mixed with the picture files he had looked at the other day. Most of the articles were from the local newspaper, which had since gone digital, allowing for quick searches. Also, the school newspaper had quite a few back issues that he obtained from the library. He quickly scanned the titles, reading some to verify the content, and then he narrowed his research to two. The whole process took him about thirty seconds. "Let's see a human teacher process data this quickly," he said, and opened the first article. It was about a tragedy at the school twenty years ago involving a teacher and a big bottle of hydrochloric acid. The whole class had to be rushed to the hospital—one student never recovered and was pronounced dead upon arriving at the emergency room. The information on the incident was vague. The student's name was Bryan, and he was a senior. *Not Cory*, Rob thought.

He went to the other article. It was about an accident five years ago involving a group of boys attempting to play a school prank. Not thinking the prank was anything but harmless, the boys proceeded to break into the building through a courtyard window. A ladder was used to gain access to the courtyard and a rock was used to gain access to a classroom. A newly hired night security guard, anxious to fulfill his duties, overreacted and hit the first boy to enter the hallway with his nightstick. The autopsy showed evidence that his death was caused by hitting his head on the corner of a locker as he fell to the ground. The boy never made it to the hospital—and the boy's name was Cory. The other boys were never charged and had since moved away. The security guard received a light sentence that involved community service and parole. He was no longer an employee of the school district and was no longer anyone's security guard.

This has to be Natalie's brother, he thought. *There must be a reason why Cory has not moved on to where spirits are supposed to move on to, and feels a need to hack into computer systems and to visit principals and substitute teachers that he never met while being alive. Natalie did say he was a good person, but then why did he think breaking into the school was a good idea?*

The next day, Rob made a point to visit the library during his planning period, which was right after lunch. The Natalie mystery would have to wait—she had not heard any more from her dead brother and had told him so during fourth period.

Upon entering the library, he found Mr. Gorman busily working at his computer. He looked up when Rob softly cleared his throat. With a wide smile, the librarian said, "Hello, you must be the new student teacher. Mr. Cooper, is it?"

"Yes," Rob answered.

"I've been expecting your visit. Mr. Ottinger tells me that you are interested in helping me secure the computer network." The smile disappeared. "I really think I have everything under control. For your knowledge, I personally designed and installed the whole system from the ground up. Tell me, Mr. Cooper, what is your experience with computer security? Have you ever heard of a SonicWall?"

"Well, no, but . . ."

"A SonicWall is an extremely effective firewall."

"Yet . . . a student or someone has found their way in." Rob paused, knowing immediately that he had offended Mr. Gorman by the shocked look on his face, just staring at him. Switching gears, Rob continued. "I don't claim to be an expert on networking, like you, but I do have some knowledge of computer languages, codes, routing tables, and such, and maybe we could put our heads together on the matter. Don't see me as a threat, but as someone who wants to work with you and learn from you."

Mr. Gorman's eyes softened, somewhat, and he spoke. "Of course. I'm sorry. It's just been frustrating and I'm running out of ideas."

"No worries. Now what were you saying about the SonicWall?"

"It's trash night, dear," Bill's wife, Leigh, reminded him as she passed going into the bedroom.

"I've already taken it out, honey," he said with a smile. "Just checking a few emails. Be in shortly."

The unread email list was lengthy—the "joys" of being a principal. Some of the emails required responses, for example, the ones from parents. Staff emails should also be dealt with, but a face-to-face chat was usually better for those. "Oh, look at the time. I gotta get to bed," he whispered and just replied, *See me tomorrow*, to all the staff emails.

Bill was only momentarily distracted when Max, the family dog, started barking in the next room. "Quiet, Max!" he demanded.

Max obeyed, and Bill went back to answering emails. *Only a few more*, he thought. Again, Max started barking and this time would not stop. "Dammit," Bill said out loud. He got up and walked into the living room where the barking, and now growling, continued. "What's the matter, boy?"

Max was in the middle of the room, barking and staring at the television, seeming unaware of Bill's presence. The television was on, no picture, only static. *Strange,* Bill thought. *I haven't seen static on a television since the days of rabbit ears.*

Bill reached for the remote on the coffee table and turned off the television. Max stopped barking. Then Bill turned the television back on with the remote. The ten o'clock news flashed onto the screen, now into the weather portion of the program. The television appeared to be working again.

"Shows over, boy, time for bed." Bill walked back to his office with Max in tow. "Got to love technology," he said.

The computer had gone to the screensaver. Bill moved the mouse, and all the emails were back, staring him in the face. *That's enough for tonight*, he thought as he reached down to give Max a scratch behind the ears.

He turned back toward his laptop to close it. The list of emails was gone. He was now staring at a black screen with a small blinking cursor. Then someone typed, *Did you miss me?* on the screen. "Please go away," Bill said in a soft voice.

NO!!! MAKE THE ROBOT GO AWAY was the reply on the screen. Bill put his hands on the keyboard and typed. *Are you one of our students?*

The screen immediately went back to his email page. Bill stared a moment, shook his head, and said, "Maybe I'm just getting senile, Max."

Max cocked his head to one side. Then Bill powered off the computer and walked upstairs to his bedroom, still shaking his head. Max followed.

The next morning on the way to school, Rob was thinking about the SonicWall firewall Mr. Gorman had shown him. It was basically a plastic blue box that was placed between the school's network and the outside world. Mr. Gorman used software to allow access to certain things and block the bad things. Most of the really bad things were already pre-programed. *Simple enough*, Rob thought, *the SonicWall should catch a hacker, unless the hacker was a ghost or a spirit of some kind? Crazy idea. The hacker was probably just one of the tech-savvy students and was using the data lines for his or her own purpose; what-ever that was. However, that did not explain the toilets flushing in the bathrooms, where there were no data lines.* Another thing that was bothering Rob was that this ghost was pestering and scaring people. *That didn't sound like the person Natalie had described. According to her, Cory would never intentionally hurt anyone. Unless just being a ghost made a person turn evil.* He pushed that thought out of his hard drive.

The day began smoothly as far as hauntings go, but not smoothly as far as being a teacher goes. Rob was asked to lead the class in a discussion about conjugating verbs. His knowledge about the mean-ing was not the problem; the problem was being able to explain it to the students. The link between Rob's brain functions and his verbal skills was questionable; it was like there were a few wires going where they weren't supposed to. Not sure how to fix it, he just tried to adapt. The adaptation was mediocre at best but got better as the periods passed. During fourth period, Rob asked Natalie, while passing her desk, if there was any more news from her brother. She just shook her head from side to side.

In the afternoon, coming back from his car, where he chose to regenerate, Rob heard a commotion coming from the back hall near the gym. He immediately turned and ran around the corner, coming face-to-face with Ms. Swenson. "I wouldn't go there, Mr. Cooper," she said. "Too much blood. I need to find Paula for the clean-up." She quickly skirted by Rob and was gone. Rob turned back to see paramedics carrying a stretcher from the boys' bathroom. There was indeed a lot of blood, but he could see the boy on the stretcher moving and talking. His voice was too low for Rob to make out. Rob hurried over and said, "Can I help?"

"All taken care of, please go back to your classrooms and get the students contained," one of the paramedics replied.

Rob did what he was told. Later, he found out that the boy—his name was Billy, and Rob had never met him before—went into the bathroom where someone pushed him face first into the urinal. It broke his nose, but he was otherwise unharmed.

Students were questioned about what they saw. Many of them heard Billy screaming, but nobody saw anyone else come out of the bathroom. Billy didn't see anyone either.

The school went into a short lockdown while the principal and a few of the school board members investigated. As it was Friday, once they had discovered all they could, everyone, Rob included, was sent home for a little extra weekend time.

"I hear the boy is recovering nicely and that he's already home," Natalie's mom said as she returned to the dinner table, sat down, and passed out the dinner rolls, the kind that come out of a can.

Natalie nodded and spread butter on the roll in front of her.

Her mom had put together a decent meal, which included most of the food groups—nothing fancy. The death of their son was devastating for both parents, and five years later, her mom was just getting back to cooking. Meals for the longest time were mostly "fend for yourself." Natalie helped as much as she could with grocery shopping and cleaning the house, but she was also going through struggles of her own.

"I really miss Cory," Natalie said, changing the subject. She had heard some rumors about what had happened at school today, but no one really knew, and the teachers weren't telling, only asking lots of questions. Billy would likely go through the rest of his high school career known as toilet head. Funny to almost everyone but not Billy.

"I know, dear," her mother answered. "We all miss him." She sighed.

"I've been having dreams about him," Natalie blurted out. "He talks to me."

"That's probably normal, dear. We dream of him as well," her dad added. "I mean, we don't want to forget him." He paused, then asked, "How is your first week back at school going?"

"Fine. There's a new student teacher in language arts; his name is Mr. Cooper."

"That's nice, dear," her mom said as she took a small bite of her potatoes.

"He's really nice, and I talked to him about Cory."

"Why would you do that, Natalie?" asked her father, sharply. Now she had both of her parents' attention. "That seems like a very odd thing to bring up to someone you just met." Her father got up from the table. "That'll be enough of that, Natalie Jean." Then he stomped off into the living room, leaving his unfinished dinner.

"Now you have upset your father, Natalie," her mom said. Then she continued with a softer voice. "We all miss Cory, but what were you thinking, dear? We need to move on."

"But you said it was good to think about him; not to forget him."

"Yes, but to yourself. This is none of this Mr. Student Teacher's business."

"His name is Mr. Cooper, and the reason I talked to him is because Cory asked me too." Her mother stared at her in disbelief and then cried.

"Natalie, your brother is dead," her mother said quietly, "and he's not coming back." Still crying, she walked over to give Natalie a hug.

"I know, Mom, but this was in a dream that I was trying to tell you about."

As her mom gathered her in a hug, something in the kitchen window caught her eye. She blinked her eyes in disbelief. It was Cory's reflection, shaking his head as if to tell her no. She let out a loud gasp, and her mom stepped back.

"Are you alright?" she asked.

"Yes, but I think I need to go to bed. You're right, Mom. I shouldn't have said anything to Mr. Cooper. I won't anymore," Natalie said, turning toward the stairs.

"Wait, Natalie—" her mom began.

"I'm fine. I'll see you in the morning," she said, hurrying upstairs. Her mother stared after her for a moment and then carried the uneaten meals to the sink.

In her room, Natalie got dressed for bed, climbed in under the covers, and looked at her window. The image of Cory did not return, and her eyelids got heavier and fell closed.

She heard a voice.

"You need to be careful who you talk to about me," Cory said as he floated above her bed. "The only one who can help is Mr. Cooper."

"Oh, Cory, I miss you so much," Natalie said, "but you're scaring me." The image of Cory reached down and touched Natalie's hair in comfort.

"You must be brave, little sis," he said. "I can't tell you everything, but you need to know that Mr. Cooper is not like the other teachers. He's like C3PO in *Star Wars*."

"That's silly, Cory. Mr. Cooper's not gold." She laughed, then it hit her. "You mean he's a robot?"

"Go to him again and tell him that the ghost haunting the school is not me."

"Then who is the ghost?" she asked.

"It's an evil spirit, a sort of demonic presence, and I know where it is." Cory looked straight into Natalie's eyes. "I came to you because I don't want you or anyone else at your school to get hurt. I'll need Mr. Cooper's help," Cory said as his image faded. "Tell him that the spirit moves through electrical and data lines and also through water. And the most important thing is that it is located down . . ." Cory's voice trailed away, and he was gone.

"Wait, I didn't catch the last part," Natalie cried as she tried to get up from the bed. But she couldn't move.

She looked to the window and saw a terrifying specter smiling back at her with sharp, yellow teeth.

She screamed and felt herself open her eyes. She was covered in a cold sweat.

It was a dream, she thought.

Natalie quickly grabbed the notebook from her nightstand and wrote down as much as she could remember, before it faded. With the weekend ahead and not being able to contact Mr. Cooper until Monday, she hoped that it would not be too late.

And she also wished she had heard the most important thing.

Rob spent most of his weekend cleaning his apartment.

Cleaning added a new challenge to his life. He knew what the vacuum was for, but he still had to download its operation manual into his hard drive to understand the whole process of plugging the cord in and to find where the on switch was located. As he vacuumed, he listened to the television, turned up high so he could hear the football game on. He was becoming fond of football and was able to pick up strategies of the game quite quickly.

Rob was about finished with the bedroom when he vaguely heard a sound coming from the front door. He turned off the vacuum, turned down the television, and listened. It was a scratching sound, coming from the front door. He opened the door and something furry raced past his feet before he realized what was happening. It was a small dog.

"Hey, get back here," he said and ran after the intruder. The dog ran up to him and put its front paws up on Rob, as if asking to be picked up. Rob did so, and the dog commenced to lick him in the face. "Who are you? I don't own a dog." Rob laughed, trying to get the dog to stop licking. He carried the dog back outside and set it down. "Go home, dog," he said. The dog did not go home but tried again to jump up.

Rob walked around, knocking on doors to ask his neighbors if this was their dog. "No, but he's cute," was the standard answer. When there were no more doors, he walked back to his own apartment with the dog following. "You can't live with me, dog." The dog only looked up at him and wagged its tail. "Okay, you can come in but only until I can find your owner."

One of his neighbors had pointed out that he—the dog was male—did not have a collar, and with no identification, it would be hard to find the owner.

"I guess if you're going to stay here, you'll need a name."

Rob did not know what a good name would be. *He was lost, so maybe I should call him 'Lost Dog,'* he thought, then he realized that maybe one word would be better. In the end, Rob named him "Lick" because that was what he wanted to do the most.

After spending a small amount of time on Google, Rob made a list of all the things he would need to keep a dog and clean up his messes, then he headed to the store. He didn't think dogs were allowed in the store, so Lick stayed in the apartment.

When Rob returned, Lick greeted him at the door with tons of licks. Rob noticed that the sun had gone down, and the apartment was dark. He made a mental note to leave a few lights on for Lick in the future. He also saw there was no sign of damage, so Lick must be used to staying alone inside. *Good thing,* he thought, *because I don't think Mr. Johnson would allow him in the classroom.*

Rob sat down on the sofa, and Lick jumped up next to him. "I wonder if I should report you to Ms. Moss or anyone else at the company?" he said.

Lick wagged his tail.

"I guess I don't need to bother them with the small matter of a small dog."

Lick jumped over onto his lap and licked his face. "Okay, boy, I like you too. We shall make a good team."

Rob saw the kitchen light turn off, and then he heard running water. Lick started barking as Rob ran in to investigate.

The faucet was running wide open. He grabbed the lever to turn it off and found that it would not move. The water continued to pour, and the dog continued to bark.

"Stop!" he yelled to the faucet, continuing to turn the lever.

Suddenly, he was able to close the valve. It was as if the faucet followed his order.

How odd, he thought. Out in the living room, the television had turned on and was blaring the local weather at full volume. Rob ran to the remote and turned down the volume. After the sound was turned all the way off, the television went black. A face suddenly appeared on the screen—not a detailed face but more of a silhouette with vague features indicating eyes, a nose, and a mouth. The head moved from side to side as if surveying the room.

Lick growled and backed away.

"Who are you?" Rob asked. The figure on the screen remained silent. "You're maybe scaring my dog, but not me." Still, there was no response. Then Rob noticed that the mouth was moving, but there was no sound, and he remembered he had just turned down the volume. The remote was still in his hand, so he turned it up.

"That's better," said the head on the screen. It cleared its throat and continued. "You should also be afraid," it said.

"And why is that, I mean, you can't even turn up the volume on the television set," Rob said with a laugh.

"STOP LAUGHING!" the figure demanded. "I *am* powerful, and I can do anything."

"Is your name Cory, by chance?"

"Cory?" The figure paused momentarily. "Yes, that's my name, and I'll take over the school and much worse if you don't go away." Rob put his finger on the remote's off button.

"You don't sound too sure about your name. Tell me, what is your sister's name?"

"Why should I tell you that? You have gone too far. Now I'm going to . . ."

"To what?" Rob interrupted. "This is my day off, and you need to get out of my apartment. He pressed the button, and the screen went black as the figure tried to yell something, but it was never heard. The television was off.

Rob sat back down on the sofa. Lick jumped up on his lap, gave a few licks, then curled up beside him to go to sleep. After about an hour with no more disturbances, Rob took Lick out to relieve himself, then showed him the new dog bed that was next to his bed. Lick curled up in it and went to sleep.

The thing on the screen is not as powerful as he claims, Rob thinks. *And I'm not sure that he is Natalie's brother.*

He then got on the bed and plugged himself in to recharge. "I can take this thing out," he said to his now-sleeping furry friend. Then he allowed himself to time out.

The next day, along with tending to Lick in the usual ways, Rob spent most of the day reexamining the clues of the case. He felt that it was going on too long, and he needed to be more aggressive. Talking to Natalie would be essential. Maybe she had some more information.

In the meantime, the internet proved to be a great source for learning how to get rid of evil spirits. A common method was to burn sage in the areas of their presence. *That seems easy enough*, he thought. *Now, where do I get some?* He found that lots of places sold sage to burn, the closest being Walmart, where he could buy a complete negative energy cleansing kit for around sixteen dollars. "Could it be this easy?" he asked Lick, who was busy sniffing the bag of dog food and not paying any attention to the question.

Soon, Rob was back from the store with all the necessary supplies for the next day. It did cross his mind whether they would let him burn sage in the school. Also, he couldn't be sure that the smoke from the sage wouldn't set off the smoke alarms and, in turn, summon the fire department. *All bridges to cross when the time comes*, he thought.

Lick jumped up on the sofa, and Rob scratched his ears until bedtime. "Tomorrow will be a big day for both of us, Lick," he said. "Me being a full-on Ghostbuster and you having to stay home alone." Rob frowned at the thought, and Lick wagged his tail, stepped onto his bed, and went to sleep. *Must be nice to be a dog and just live for the moment.*

"Good night, boy," he said and turned off the lights.

The next morning, Rob grabbed his coat, walked to the door, and paused when he felt something tug at the cuff of his pants. It was Lick wagging his tail. "Sorry, boy, I have to go now."

Rob knelt down and scratched Lick behind the ears. "I wish you could go with me, but there's a rule about dogs in school, unfortunately." He gave Lick one more pat on the head, told him he would be back later, and left the apartment.

It was going to be a long day. His plan was to come back during his lunch break to take Lick for a walk—he really needed to find one of the neighbors willing to do this. He stood outside the door, listening for a short while. No sound from Lick. *What a good boy*, Rob thought.

There was a lot on his mind on the way to school that morning.

On the seat next to him was the sage kit from Walmart, along with a lighter wand. He had decided not to ask for permission to light the sage. If you ask and are denied, then it limits your options. The big questions remaining were, where should he light the sage, and where was the spirit's main room in the school? The clues he was dealing with now gave him zero indications. He could sage the whole school, one room at a time. But then he would need more time and the chances of getting caught would be great. What he needed was more information from Natalie.

"Come on, Cory, help us out," he said aloud.

He walked into the school with the sage concealed in a grocery bag and headed to the teachers' lounge to hide it on a coatrack, placing his coat on top. With his ever-present coffee thermos, he went straight to the classroom. Mr. Johnson was already sitting at his desk with the week's lesson plans in front of him. "Good morning, Rob. How was your weekend?" he said.

"Very relaxing, no visits from evil beings."

Mr. Johnson gave him a strange look.

"I mean, it was just a normal weekend. Oh, I have a dog now, and his name is Lick."

"That doesn't sound like a very normal weekend," Mr. Johnson said. "Lick? That's a funny name," he chuckled.

Darn, what is a normal name for a dog? Rob thought. "He likes to lick a lot, so it seemed appropriate."

"I guess that makes sense, sort of. Anyway, this is the week you're to take over the class as the main teacher. I prepared the lesson plans for this week. Next week, I'll have you write them." He handed the plans to Rob, who went to the back of the room to look them over at his desk. They seemed straightforward: discussions on the *Old Man and the Sea*, a few grammar lessons along with worksheets, and a test at the end of the week. He would need to make the worksheet copies in the teachers' lounge during his break.

Rob kept staring at the plans for a while, even though he had them memorized in seconds. One of the perks of having a computer for a brain.

The class discussions went smoothly, and he found it satisfying to be the one in charge even though Mr. Johnson was still in the room observing. Rob knew the story inside and out and was able to add additional insight to the discussion questions that were given to him. In fact, he was so enthralled that for a while he completely forgot about his mission to rid the school of the evil presents and about talking to Natalie. It came back to him when, during fourth period, he looked at her and saw her mouthing something to him. Reading lips was not one of his skills, so he just nodded his head to indicate he knew she had news.

After the grammar lesson was taught and the worksheets were handed out, he walked up to Natalie's desk.

"I heard from Cory. He gave me some more clues," she said, and handed Rob a folded piece of paper. "That's what I remember from my dream. The bad thing is he had something 'really important' to tell me and I didn't get that part." Then a big smile appeared on her face, and she said, "He also came to me before I went to sleep as a reflection in a window, but I don't think he could talk to me that way."

Rob quickly read her note. The message validated what Rob was already figuring out. Cory was trying to help, and he was not the evil spirit. "I'm guessing that 'the really important thing' that he was referring to was where in the school was its' main hideout. I know where I want to look first. Can you help me after school?"

"Yes, I'll call my parents and tell them I'm going to stay over with my girlfriend and work on a school project," she said.

"Okay, good. I have one place I want to investigate first, and that's the library," Rob said. "I'll fill you in on what I think after school. I think that I'm finally starting to connect the dots." Rob walked back up to the front of the classroom, the bell rang, and he dismissed the class. Natalie had a big smile as she left the room.

During his lunch break, Rob enjoyed his short time with Lick and was yet again saddened to have to say goodbye. If there was only a way that he could go to school. On the way back to school, he searched for a solution and found one. A service dog! That was the solution. Service dogs could go anywhere. He had seen the signs on store entry doors that read "No Pets Allowed Except Service Animals," and a dog is an animal. *Perfect*, he thought.

As the last bell of the day was ringing, Rob was gathering his books and heading out the door toward the teachers' lounge. Miss Swenson was sitting at the lounge table, eating an apple. "Well, you're a sight for sore eyes," she said. "The person I need to talk to."

"Me? Why?" Rob headed over to the coatrack.

"Well, as I was sitting here, a coat fell off the rack. You know, I thought it was an odd thing, no one else was in the room and, of course, no wind." She chuckled. "As I was hanging it back up, I noticed a grocery bag on the hook. I didn't mean to be nosy, but it was giving off a strange smell, so I peeked inside and I found that it contained sage, and there's only one use for that, that I know of—ridding spirits." She paused, looking for a reaction, and got nothing from Rob. "Is this yours? It was behind your jacket, you know."

Not knowing exactly what to say, Rob just gave a puzzled look, looked inside the bag, and answered, "I saw the bag when I hung up my jacket but didn't look inside. Ridding spirits, you said?"

"Oh yes, and mostly evil spirits. I don't know what happens to the good spirits, but they probably don't like the smell either." She walked over, bent down, and grabbed his jacket. "Don't forget this," she said. "I'll take the bag to the principal."

"That's okay, I can take it to him."

"No, I can, no problem," she said as she grabbed the grocery bag and left the room. Leaving Rob standing there, wondering what to do next. Natalie would be waiting for him in the library, and if his hunch was correct, he would be in the presence of the spirit without a weapon. He put his jacket back on the empty hook and headed to the library.

Natalie was waiting for him. She had a strange look on her face. "Mr. Cooper, do you like *Star Wars*?" she asked.

"The movie? Yes, I guess so," was his answer, not sure where she was going with this.

Her smile broadened. "Me too. My favorite character in the movie is C3P0. He's a very funny and likable robot," she said. "Kind of like you."

Rob wasn't sure if she was referring to his wit and charm or to the fact of him being a robot. *How could she have found out?* he thought. *I've been so clever at fitting in.* "Like me? That's silly." Rob gave a slightly uncomfortable laugh.

"Cory told me, in my dream," she said. "But don't worry, your secret is safe with me. I won't tell anyone. Anyway, who would believe me?"

Realizing his identity had been discovered, he said, "Cory was right. I guess the good thing about this is that everything else he told you is probably right too. Come on! We have an evil spirit to find." He walked past her into the library, trying to show his courage but wishing that he still had the sage.

Paula was at the far end of the library, dusting the tops of the computers. Most of the research was conducted through the internet, and the stacks of books were in more need of dusting than the computers. Rob cleared his throat, and Paula, not expecting anyone to be in the library, jumped and let out a soft scream. "Oh my, you startled me."

"We're sorry, Paula," Rob said. "We were just wanting to look around—maybe try to find the source of the spooky guy that you talked about."

"Good luck on that, but I think you're wasting your time," she said and finished dusting the last computer. She turned around, grabbed the handle of her cleaning cart, and headed to the exit. "I'm always glad to get this room finished. Thank goodness for Mr. Gorman being a coach and leaving during the last period. The previous librarian had a class in here at the end of the day, and a lot of the time he and his students stayed late to finish up their projects," she sighed. "It was horrible coming in here after dark. I almost quit."

"I'm so glad you didn't quit. The school wouldn't be the same without you," Rob said, then added. "I *am* curious, however. What class did the other librarian teach?"

"Photography," Paula answered. "The students took pictures and then developed the prints in the darkroom right here in the library. Some of their pictures won awards on a national level, they tell me."

"How interesting," said Natalie, stepping beside Rob. "I didn't know the school had a darkroom. Where is it?"

"Oh well, you can't get to it anymore, it's been walled up," Paula said. "I guess no one wanted to be reminded about the accident. Such a tragedy, and probably the reason that the librarian was fired. His name was Mr. French, and everyone loved him, but he was careless, and when you're working with chemicals, you shouldn't be careless."

"How horrible," said Rob. "What happened? Was anyone hurt?"

"Yes, one of the students in the photography class. It didn't surprise most—he was not one to follow the rules." Paula looked toward the library office and shook her head. "But still a tragic loss."

"Was his name Bryan?" Rob asked, remembering the article about an accident involving hydrochloric acid and a death in the school. The article had not provided much information.

Paula scrunched her nose and looked up as if the answer was going to be on the ceiling, then answered. "I believe his name was Bryan. How did you know?"

"I was looking at articles about the school's local history, and I came across an article about the accident. Not much was written about it, however." The article made no mention of a darkroom or the fact that a teacher was fired. Rob made a mental note to ask Mr. Ottinger about Mr. French.

"Where exactly was the darkroom located?" Natalie asked.

"There were two doors: one at the back of Mr. Gorman's office and another that opened into the hallway. Both have been sealed off. You can't even tell there was ever a door there—at least in the hallway. Not as good of a job in the office," Paula said.

"Paula, would it be possible for us to see the spot where the door was sealed off in the office?" Rob asked, not knowing if Paula had access to the office door that he assumed was locked.

"Oh, sure. The door is not locked," she said as if reading his mind. "The lock is broken and needs to be fixed." Paula walked to the door, pushed it open, turned on the lights, and walked inside. "Come on in," she said, and Rob and Natalie followed.

The concealed door was around the backside of a bookshelf that contained old back issues of periodicals that, because of the internet, were seldom used and were covered with dust. Paula was right. Apparently, there was hardly any effort to seal off the darkroom from this side. A single piece of plywood was put in place with screws. They didn't even bother to paint the plywood.

Hanging near it was a poster of a famous actor holding a book and the word "READ" across the top. Someone, probably a student, had hastily written, "I don't think he can" next to the picture. Which is why the poster had been retired to the far end of the office to never be seen again—except by the librarian, who saw the humor.

Rob reached out and touched the wood concealing the hidden darkroom. A strange vibration, almost a slight current, shot up his arm, and he snapped his hand back.

"Something wrong?" Paula said and stepped back away from the hidden doorway.

"No. I think I just got a splinter from the wood." Rob pretended to pull the imaginary splinter from his finger. He looked at Natalie and made a slow nod. She nodded back to let him know she understood. This was the place where the evil spirit was residing. The only place in the school where no one could enter. "Thank you for showing me this," he said.

Paula smiled, and Rob followed her out of the door and back into the library.

He thanked her again and they made their way into the main hallway, where Rob ran directly into Mr. Ottinger. The principal immediately held up a grocery bag, pushing it into Rob's face. "Is this yours? You don't need to answer because I know it is." He looked into the bag and lowered his voice. "I know what this is and what it is used for," he said. "Miss Swenson just gave this to me and said it was behind your jacket but that you didn't know where it came from."

"I didn't want her to be suspicious of what we were going to—"

Mr. Ottinger cut him off mid-sentence and shoved the bag into Rob's hands. "Just take it," he whispered. Then turned to walk away "And don't set off the fire alarms," he added, and left Rob there holding the bag.

Rob looked at Natalie, shrugged his shoulders, and said, "Maybe we should come back tomorrow and finish the job. Unless you're up for it now."

"Let's get this over with," she said. "My mom thinks I'm staying at a girlfriend's house, so I have all night."

Rob smiled. "Let's give Paula time to finish cleaning in there, and then we will take care of Bryan."

"Sounds like a plan," she said, and reached into her backpack to pull out a roll of tape. She tore off a piece and covered up the hole in the doorjamb. "To prevent the door from locking," she said.

"Not your first rodeo?" Rob asked.

Natalie smiled. "I saw this in a movie once."

She dropped the tape back into her backpack and they walked down the hall, waiting for Paula to leave the library.

When she didn't appear, Rob went to investigate only to find that she had gone out one of the other doors. "I guess she never planned on locking this door. Good to know."

Suddenly, down the hallway, someone yelled, "Call a plumber! We're being flooded!"

Rob looked. It was true. The hall was being flooded, and it was coming out of the boy's bathroom.

"It's Bryan," Natalie said. "He knows what we're up to, and he's causing a distraction. Cory told me he can also travel through water."

"I think you're right."

Rob ran down the hall and into the bathroom, where he found that all the faucets were turned on full blast, the sinks were not draining, and the water was gushing over the sides. He quickly turned each faucet off. *Problem solved and without a plumber*, he thought.

He turned to leave. Then he noticed something floating in the water.

It was the grocery bag. He had accidentally dropped it while turning off the faucets, and now the contents had all come out and were wet. *I'll bet that a wet stick of sage will not light*, he thought. He would have to go back to Walmart for some more. They would have to continue the mission another day.

When he returned to the hallway and reported back to Natalie about the change in plans, she told him her mother probably wouldn't want her to stay over at a girlfriend's house two nights in a row. The next day, Rob would be on his own.

Rob headed straight home and walked and fed Lick, then he drove to Walmart to pick up another sage kit. While he was at the store, he searched the pet section for service dog vests. He found a wide assortment of vests, none saying "service dog," however.

"Can I help you?" said a young girl, wearing a light blue Walmart vest of her own.

"Yes, where do you keep the service dog vests?"

"You have to order those online. You'll need to get your dog registered as a service dog first," she said.

"No, I don't have time for that," Rob said. "I was hoping to get one today. Thanks, anyway."

As Rob walked away, the young girl added, "We do have a comfort dog vest here at the store. You don't need to register for those—I don't think."

Comfort dog! That's it. Lick was born to give comfort. "Yes," he said. "That'll be perfect."

Rob brought home the new vest, which was bright red, slightly too big, and said, "COMFORT DOG—PLEASE PET ME." Lick loved it.

"You need to go to bed, boy. Tomorrow is a big day—your first day at school and you can help me rid the school of evil spirits."

Lick cocked his head.

"Never mind, I'll just need your moral support."

The next day, Lick drew lots of attention from the students and a few strange looks from the other teachers as Rob walked him down the hallway to his classroom. "What's his name?" was a common question, and lots of laughs when Rob told them. "Cute dog—stupid name," said one of the girls.

"Don't listen to her, boy," he whispered. But it was obvious that Lick didn't care what his name was. He was having the time of his life, as evident by his tail going about one hundred miles an hour.

Along with the leash, Rob also carried a reusable grocery bag containing a dog dish, a few dog treats, the sage kit, and a screwdriver to remove the screws from the plywood. He was not going to make the mistake again of hanging it in the teachers' lounge.

Mr. Johnson looked down at Lick and then up at Rob. "You brought your dog?"

"Yes, but he can be here now. He's a comfort dog."

"And did you tell Mr. Ottinger?"

It never occurred to Rob that Mr. Ottinger would need to know. "No," he answered. "Should I?"

"My guess is that he already knows. After all, you didn't come down the hallway quietly," Mr. Johnson said as he shook his head and went to sit down at the back of the room.

Mostly, Lick wasn't too much of a distraction during classes. He spent most of the time sleeping on Rob's jacket on the floor in the back of the room. Mr. Johnson even leaned over and scratched Lick's ears from time to time.

During fourth period, Natalie was totally enthralled by Lick. So much so that they both forgot about what the plans were after school. She did, however, confirm that she couldn't stay on account of her mother having caught her in yesterday's lie when she called her girlfriend's house and found she was not there.

"I'll call her after school and see if I can change her mind," she said. "I'll say that I need to work on a project and that I'll be home as soon as I finish. I'll meet you at the library, if I'm able to work it out with my mother."

"I'll keep my fingers crossed," Rob said.

Lick turned out to be a very good student. Most of the time, Rob forgot he was in the classroom, and he only needed to go outside a couple of times.

After all the students and Mr. Johnson had left the room for the day, Rob spent time at his desk grading papers. He figured that Paula would be cleaning the library for about forty-five minutes. Then he could go in, remove the plywood, and burn the sage.

When it was time to go, Rob put the leash on Lick and grabbed the bag, holding everything he needed. Rob searched the hallways that led to the library in hopes of finding Natalie. Of course, he could burn the sage without her, but it would be nice to have someone to look after Lick. But Natalie did not show up, so he continued with his plan.

The library door was unlocked. He walked in with Lick and shut the door behind them, then took off Lick's leash. "You may need to get away if there's any trouble."

Lick licked his hand as if understanding the situation.

Rob walked through the partially lit room and opened the door into the back room. This room was dark, so he turned on the light before walking around the big bookshelf to the piece of bare plywood. He reached inside his bag and grabbed the screwdriver and the small flashlight, which he put into his pocket.

As Rob started to turn the first screw, he heard a low gravelly noise. He jumped back, and the noise continued, but not from behind the plywood. It was coming from Lick, whose neck hairs were standing up. His nose was wrinkled, and his teeth were clenched in a snarl.

"What's the matter, boy?" he asked, then realized he already knew the answer. Lick could sense the evil spirit behind the board. "It's OK," he told Lick as he reached to smooth down the hairs on the dog's neck.

It took a few minutes for Lick to calm down enough that Rob

could continue taking out the screws. It was a slow process and made Rob wish he had brought a drill. After the last screw was removed, Rob said, "Let's take a look," and pulled the board back.

A regular person's eyes would have taken time to adjust to the level of light inside the room, but Rob's eyes adjusted immediately. He could see a counter with lots of trays and a sink and wires strung from one side of the room to the other. From what he knew about darkrooms, this looked set up and ready for developing pictures.

Something touched Rob's leg, and he jumped, startling Lick, who was the cause. "Sorry, Lick," he said and continued his investigation.

He found a light switch and clicked it on. A dusty red lightbulb came to life above the counter. He thought it was strange that they didn't bother to disconnect the power. Next, he tried the faucet—water gushed into the sink. *This could still be a working darkroom,* he thought.

Rob removed the sage and the lighter from the bag, stuffing the empty bag into his back pocket. He clicked the trigger on the lighter and was putting the sage up to the flame when he heard a voice behind him. "Bad idea, Mr. Robot."

Rob turned. No one was there, just a wall and the shut door that led back into the library office. *There wasn't a door before*, he thought.

He turned all the way around. Now he was in an enclosed room, which was dark except for the red glow from the bulb overhead, and it had two doors. *Yes, it was supposed to have two doors,* he thought, *one from the library office and one to exit to the hallway.* He tried the office door first and found that it was locked. Rob then walked over to the other door and turned the knob—it was not locked.

"Follow me, Lick," he said and looked around the room.

Lick was not there. Lick was gone.

"Lick! Come!" he yelled.

Rob turned the doorknob again and pulled the door open. The hall was full of students walking, talking to one another, and the strangest thing was that they didn't appear to notice him. Also, he didn't recognize any of the students and the clothes they were wearing were different from what he was used to seeing. He heard a soft yip from down the hall to his right. It was Lick, who was being held by the collar by a boy dressed in ragged jeans and a T-shirt that hadn't seen the inside of a washer in decades. The boy was smiling.

"Welcome to my world," he said.

"Let go of my dog, Bryan," Rob said. "I'm here to help you."

"Don't lie, you are here to get rid of me."

The other students in the hall continued to walk and talk to each other but seemed unaware of either Rob or Bryan. "These students, they don't see us," Rob said and reached out to touch one of the boys who was walking close by. His hand passed through him.

"They aren't real," Bryan said. "They are my memories, and this is my Hell." Bryan looked down at Lick. "I like this dog—he can actually see me. It's lonely in here and so boring."

"I want to help you," Rob repeated. "Why is it that you are here? Why are you causing trouble for the school?"

"Why shouldn't I? They caused me trouble, and now I'm doomed to walk these halls. Once I figured out that I could travel through the electrical lines and the waterlines, I'm not as bored. I'm having fun!" Bryan got up, forgetting about Lick, who immediately ran over to Rob, went around him, and stuck his head out between his ankles.

"What happened to you was an accident," Rob said.

"Is that what you think?" Bryan said, moving toward Rob. "An accident! Who do you think knocked over the bottle of acid?"

The article had not gone into much detail about what had happened. "Tell me," Rob said.

"I did it!" he yelled. "I hated this school and how everyone treated me. I was going to make them pay by burning down the school, by setting the hydrochloric acid on fire in the hallway. But my hands were wet, and the bottle fell and broke. The fumes were overwhelming, and the next thing I remember was being here in the hallway—not able to leave—and it was years before I realized that I was dead. Now I'll make everyone pay."

"I want to help, but I can't let you do this," Rob said and held up the sage and lighter that were still in his hands. He walked toward Bryan, who lunged forward and knocked everything out of Rob's hands. The sage and the lighter went skidding across the hallway floor. Bryan slammed into Rob with such force that he lost his balance and fell to the hard tile floor.

"Now to deactivate you, Mr. Robot," Bryan said, crouching down and taking hold of Rob's neck.

Rob's vision was slowly fading as Bryan squeezed the circuits located in his neck. He could hear Lick barking behind him. *This is it*, he thought. *I failed at my first and only job.*

"Let go of him," said a familiar voice. Bryan released his grip and looked up.

It was Natalie, and she was holding the sage, which was already lit on fire and smoking.

"Stay away from me with that, or I'll . . ."

"Or you'll what?" Natalie interrupted. "My brother says you are an evil spirit, and this is how we get rid of evil spirits." She shoved the burning sage into Bryan's face, causing him to first scream and turn away. Natalie brought the smoke close to his head. He turned around suddenly and swatted the sage stick from her hand. It went flying down the hall.

"Not so tough now, are you?" he said.

He grabbed her by the shoulders and brought her face close to his, which was contorted into a monstrous snarl.

Smoke was coming up around his head, and he screamed again. Natalie looked down, and there was Lick with the sage stick in his mouth. She reached for it and shoved it into Bryan's open mouth.

Natalie watched as Bryan's body transfigured into smoke that mingled with that of the sage. All his limbs convulsed as he tried to remove the stick of sage, but he wasn't able to. As his body gave up the fight, the image of Bryan faded into a transparent image of his former self. At the very end, he became smoke and drifted away.

Natalie kneeled beside Rob, who was now sitting up with Lick licking his face. "Are you alright?" she said.

"Yes, thank you," Rob said. "You came after all."

"Sorry I was late. Needed to run an errand for my mother first. That was part of her deal to let me stay late at school today." She helped Rob up, and the three of them walked through the door into the darkroom. Inside the room, the red light was still glowing. The door to the library office was replaced by the opening Rob had created when he removed the plywood. When they looked back to the other door, the door that had gone into the hallway, it was gone.

They walked out into the library office, turned off the lights, and then left the library. Natalie suddenly stopped, turned around, and looked at her reflection in the dark library window. There, right beside her, was Cory's reflection looking back at her. She waved to him, and he blew her a kiss and faded away. She turned and walked silently with Rob and Lick down the deserted hallway.

They said their goodbyes in the parking lot where Natalie's girl-friend was waiting to drive her home. She quickly gave Rob a hug and jumped into the car, and rode away.

"Let's go home, boy," Rob said to Lick, who was wagging his tail. They got into the car and drove away.

The next morning, as he was walking through the parking lot, Rob heard a voice calling his name. "Rob, wait up." It was Ms. Susan Moss from the company.

Rob hadn't seen her since his first day on the job. "Hi, Ms. Moss, I was just going to contact you."

"We're pleased that your first job was a success," she said.

"What? How did you know? I haven't told anyone," Rob said.

"We have been keeping track of your progress," Susan said. "You are to be commended, even though you broke the rules and told the young girl, Natalie, of your mission. This will be corrected, so no harm was done."

"What do you mean by 'corrected?'" Rod didn't like the sound of this.

Ignoring the question, she continued. "The institution will be finalizing your termination of employment, and we wish you well in the future. Sufficient funds will be transferred to assist in your finding employment elsewhere—that is, if you choose to remain in a functioning state."

"Wait! What? I completed the mission successfully, now I'm ready for the next."

"Sorry, Rob Cooper, you were basically an experiment. A success in some ways and a failure in others. Your model is being replaced by newer technology. You made mistakes, and we advertise, 'robots don't make mistakes.'" She turned Rob around, opened the compartment at the back of his neck, and inserted a flash drive. "There'll be no more need for flash drives with the new model."

She turned him back around. "You'll remember parts of what happened, but not everything. Those who knew you to be a robot will no longer remember." She patted him on the shoulder and said, "Do not contact the agency—if you do, they'll be forced to terminate you permanently." She smiled and said, "Have a nice day, Rob," and walked away.

Rob walked into the building in a daze. His mind was spinning, and his thoughts were running together. Someone said something to him, but he was not able to comprehend for a response. "Are you alright?" the voice asked again. Someone helped him into the office and into a chair.

"I feel funny," Rob answered. "Maybe I should go home." He tried to get up off the chair but was forced to sit back down.

"Just rest for a moment, Mr. Cooper." It was Mr. Ottinger.

Seeing the commotion this was causing, Mr. Ottinger helped Rob into his office, sat him down, and shut the door. "Mrs. Olsteen is informing Mr. Johnson that you won't be in today."

"I finished the mission," Rob said in a dazed voice.

"What? What mission?" asked Mr. Ottinger. "Maybe I should call an EMT."

What was it that Ms. Moss had said to him just a few minutes ago? Something about people not remembering. "No need for that, Mr. Ottinger," Rob said. "I'm starting to feel better."

"Good enough to drive?"

Rob jumped to his feet. "Yes, I think I can drive."

Amazed at the quick recovery, Mr. Ottinger watched Rob exit his office and sprint outside to the parking lot. "What an odd young man," Mr. Ottinger said quietly and went back to his desk. He looked at his daily schedule on his laptop and was about to leave for his morning meeting when a brochure caught his eye. The brochure read, "Robot Investigator for Hire." "What will they think of next? How ridiculous," he said and tossed the brochure into his trash can, as he looked out the window at Rob climbing into his car.

Rob hurried home, keeping the car's speed just slow enough not to get pulled over. He parked and ran to his door. Excited to see him come back so early, Lick jumped around in circles and barked loudly. Rob calmed him down with a few ear scratches and some treats, and then he went to his desk and opened the side drawer. Inside the drawer, he found a bright red flash drive labeled "BACKUP MEMORY." Being afraid that he might forget something, Rob had run a backup of his memory banks every morning while brewing his coffee. It was easy through the opening in his wrist.

When the process was complete, and he could again fully remember, he sat down at the kitchen table. *I no longer have a job,* he thought. *What will I do?* Then it occurred to him that he still did have a job, and an important one as well. "I *am* a student teacher!" he yelled, and Lick again ran around the room barking.

Having only his own classroom to worry about, without all the ghost stuff, Rob became an excellent teacher. He still made mistakes but figured that made him appear more human. Natalie became just one of the regular students, and Rob kept it that way even though he wondered if she still had conversations with her dead brother. His guess was that she couldn't remember any of those conversations either.

One Friday morning in late December, as he was leaving school, Mr. Ottinger called Rob into his office. The first semester was ending, and so was his student teacher gig. He figured that this was what the principal wanted to talk to him about, but this was not the case.

"Rob, you have grown into an excellent teacher. In fact, probably faster than I've ever seen before," said Mr. Ottinger.

"Thank you, sir," he said. "I've loved being at Four Oaks High School and will sadly miss coming here every day." Rob dropped his head and stared at the floor.

"Yes," Mr. Ottinger said. "Well, you may not need to miss coming here."

Rob was confused and looked up.

"Mr. Johnson has decided to retire after this school year. Says he really enjoyed the extra time he had after you took over his classes. Of course, you'll still need to go through the application process. But between you and me, the job is yours if you want it."

"Thank you, Mr. Ottinger," he said. "Of course I'll have to think about this." Since he was able to think quicker than most, after a few seconds, he said, "I'd love to teach here full time! When can I start the application process?"

Rob was hired.

He went to school every day with a hot mug of coffee in hand that he discretely poured into the sink on his way to his classroom. *It's great having a steady job with a steady income*, he thought. *But if this ever falls through, I will be a detective.*

The Crawl Space

DURING MY MORNING COFFEE, my cell chimed, indicating a text from Carl. "On my way," it said.

Carl only lived a few miles from me and would be driving up my driveway soon. Bring a flashlight, he had said, so I quickly rummaged through the junk drawer and found a small penlight, clicked it on and off to see if it had working batteries, and put it into my front jeans pocket. After a short debate about whether I should have a second cup of coffee or not, I drained the last few drops, put the empty cup into the sink, and headed toward the door. This was my usual day off, in which I would normally find things around the house in need of repair. I always had the time for household projects but seldom had the money for parts. Therefore, Carl agreed to find some side jobs for me to earn extra cash. For the most part, the jobs had been easy enough, and he paid me well. All I knew about today's job was that I would need a flashlight.

Carl pulled up into my driveway in a bright red GMC Denali pickup truck. The windows were down, and country music was disturbing the otherwise peaceful morning. "Morning, Pete," he said, taking a big swig from his coffee thermos. "Great day to not be working, What's wrong with us?"

"I was just thinking the same thing," I said as I hopped in the truck and shut the door. "What's on the docket for today?"

"The easiest job so far," he replied and backed out onto the main road. "There's a drainpipe that needs to be angled so that it will drain properly—stupid plumbers," he added.

"Okay, but why the flashlight?"

"The pipe's in the crawl space."

I recoiled. "Ahhh, no, I can't do that. Is there something else?"

"Ahh, no, get over it," was his reply. Annoyed by his response and unable to think of any way to get out of this horrid task, I decided to check emails on my cell. We were silent the rest of the trip until he pulled the truck into a short driveway and turned off the engine.

"It's only a crawl space, Peter," Carl said as we exited the truck, parked next to the new construction of a rather large but unfinished house. Carl's future house.

Carl was my brother-in-law by marriage to my sister and was the CEO of a small construction company that he named Carl's Castles, Inc. He didn't want to pull his crew off other main projects to work on personal ones, so this house was falling behind schedule. "Besides," he continued, "you won't be in there for more than a few hours, four tops."

His words didn't sound very reassuring.

As I walked around to the back of the truck, the cement-gray foundation walls leered back at me. "When I asked for something to do to earn some extra cash, I didn't think you would have me crawling around with bugs in the dirt under your house. Besides," I said, "I've always been a little claustrophobic when it comes to small, dark places. Isn't there something else . . . ?"

"Sorry, Pete," he said with a smile. "Take it or leave it. I'd do it myself, but I really need to get back to my crew over on Timber Bluff. You know what they say about what happens when the cat's away." He reached into the back of his pickup and handed me a shovel, then I followed him down a short embankment to an opening in the foundation. "Besides, it's really an easy job. Stop fretting."

I investigated the opening and could not see very far because of the lack of light and what appeared to be dust floating everywhere. The flooring above had the standard 1/8 inch gaps that were letting in some light. Carl saw my concerned face. "Your eyes will adjust once you have been in there for a few seconds, I promise."

"Is there even enough room to crawl around?" I asked.

"It will be a little tight," Carl admitted. "You'll have twelve to eighteen inches between the dirt and the floor joist—give or take."

"The floor what?" I was lacking in my construction terminology.

Carl rolled his eyes. "Seriously, dude. The horizontal boards that hold up the actual flooring. It doesn't matter. Just know that you'll have enough room to easily scoot back there to the far wall and angle the drainpipe. Although you'll probably have to stay on your back and pull and push yourself with your hands and feet."

"You've got to be kidding," I said. "Surely there's another way in that's closer to the pipe."

"No, this is the only way in for now. Later, I'll probably put a trapdoor in one of the closets." Carl leaned over and moved a few of the larger tumbleweeds blocking the entrance. "Maybe you could also level some of the higher spots of dirt. Don't forget your flashlight."

"I'm not sure I can do this, Carl." I could almost feel a panic attack coming on.

"Look, I'd have done this simple task myself before, but you asked me for a way to earn some extra cash. Now I don't have time." He looked down at the opening to the crawl space. "Here's what I can do. I can add a couple hundred more to what I told you. What do you say?"

I took a deep breath to settle down my nerves. "Okay, I'll give it a try," I said, which immediately brought back the panic. I took more deep breaths.

"Great, I'll be back in a few hours to check on you." He patted me on the back and walked up the incline, then got into his truck and drove off.

I checked to make sure the flashlight was still in my pocket, grabbed my shovel, and looked into the opening. There wasn't much to see through the darkness. The damp, musty smell reminded me of a Styrofoam container full of half-moldy earthworms—the kind you use for fishing. I tried to think about other things, more pleasant things, like the extra money that Carl had promised me. I took one more deep breath, rested on my back, and scooted into the opening. Using my arms and legs, I pulled and pushed myself toward the back wall. I didn't get too far before I noticed the clearance between the dirt tend the joists was so small that I would not be able to continue much further. Maneuvering my body, I was able to move small amounts of dirt to open the gap. It was a slow process. This also kicked up plumes of dust so thick I could barely see the light filtering in from the flooring above. The sight reminded me of the black-and-white vampire movies I watched at night with my brother.

My eyes were already becoming irritated from the dust. I tried wiping them with my hand, but that just made it worse. Retrieving the flashlight from my pocket, I surveyed the area through squinted, watering eyes. I could barely see the drainpipe in question about thirty feet from where I was lying. *This is going to take some time to get there*, I thought.

I reached into my other pocket for my cell and found it empty. "Damn," I said aloud. *I must have set it down in Carl's truck.*

I restarted my mission, then stopped when something crawled across my nose. I smacked my face and hit my nose on a floor joist and cried out in pain, but there was no one to hear me. I just knew there would be bugs down here in this damp, dark hellhole.

I just needed to keep going and get this horrendous task over with.

I was able to get under the first few joists with a minor amount of shovel work. It was a slow process. After what seemed an eternity, I aimed my flashlight again at the back wall. Strange, now it seemed to be further away. *That's impossible*, I thought, and shivered.

But it seemed to be true. In fact, the more I moved toward the wall, the further away the back wall seemed, until it got to the point where the whole room looked more than twice its original size. This was definitely creepy and not worth the money.

I had one thought: *I need to get out.*

With regained energy generated from panic, I reversed my direction and began going back toward the opening—but where was it?

I looked around frantically, disoriented.

Then, I felt a sudden wave of relief. There the opening was, quite a ways away but at least I could now see it.

Deep breaths, Peter, I told myself.

That helped.

With a steadier heartbeat, I scooted toward the opening and immediately ran into a joist. The gap between the floor and the bottom of the joist here seemed to be less than a foot. *Impossible,* I thought. I just came this way. *It's like the house is trying to keep me here.* But that was ridiculous, so I shook the thought out of my head.

I still had my shovel and tried to dig at the dirt—it was like cement. Yet a moment ago, it was soft dirt. My heart once again increased in speed.

I swiveled my head back toward the wall—still a ways away, but the path was more open. In fact, it looked like I could probably crawl all the way there because the gap was now at least three feet.

Gathering my wits and keeping my flashlight aimed at the far wall, I got to my knees and crawled. To go faster, I put the flashlight into my pocket and used the shovel for support. I wanted to get the hell out of here.

Everything was extra dusty and dark, but I could see enough to tell the far wall was not getting any closer. *What's wrong with my head?* I thought. *This doesn't make any sense.*

Panic started setting in.

Then, out of the corner of my eyesight, something moved, and I heard a groan like that of an old man trying to get up from a sofa. Looking around, I saw nothing but dim shadows and lingering dust—but no, there *was* something, at the side wall to my right.

It appeared to be a small round object—about the size of a basketball but not completely round. It fell to one side, then righted itself again.

I retrieved my flashlight from my pocket and aimed the light at the strange figure. The shape moved catlike to avoid the beam.

Then it stopped.

A helpless terror ran through my body when the figure came into view. It appeared to be a human head, but greenish in color. It had short dark hair to match its dark eyes—maddening eyes, glaring at me with the thirst of a famished wolf. Then a sinister grin appeared, and it spoke with a gravelly voice. "Don't tell anyone that you saw me, Peter, or I'll find you and kill you."

My mind was racing, and déjà vu hit me like a truck. This all seemed familiar . . . but I couldn't understand why. Having never been alone in a dark crawl space and never coming face-to-face with a live detached human head before, this feeling seemed bizarre. And it knew my name.

The head reared backward as if looking up at the sky and immediately started rolling toward me.

Screaming at the top of my lungs, I turned and headed toward the back wall. I could hear the head grunting behind me. Then, taking the shovel in both hands, I turned, and there was nothing, nothing behind me but the tracks I had made. Scouring all ends of the room, I saw only darkness and dust. *Imagination is a terrible thing when you are alone in a crawl space,* I thought.

I needed to get out of here, fast, but the way I had come was now not an option—a huge mound of dirt was blocking the way. How it got there, I could not fathom.

Maybe there is another way.

Something else crawled across my face. This time, I just let it be.

The dust settled slightly, and I could see the drainpipe that was my original destination. Just a normal PVC drainpipe with what looked to be a hand crawling on top. It *actually* was a dismembered and hairy hand walking along the pipe, not using its fingers as legs, like "Thing" in *The Addams Family*, but rather using its fingers to pull itself along the pipe.

My thoughts were spinning. First the green head, now the hairy hand. *Still my imagination?*

It must be—because at that instant, I realized why the sight of the green head seemed so familiar. It and the hand were both fears from my childhood. My brother used to scare me about the hairy hand and the green head that he said lived in our basement. Even when I got older, I hated to go downstairs by myself. And now they have come back, appearing real and not just in my mind.

I'm in a nightmare, I thought, *and I need to wake.*

Closing my eyes, I could still hear the disturbing sound of the fingers on the pipe and then on the dirt getting closer and closer.

I screamed "No!" at the top of my lungs, and when all the air had left my lungs, I took a breath and opened my eyes, finding I was once more alone—no creepy hand, or green head, in my sight.

"Carl, where are you!" I yelled.

What did Carl say? Was he coming back in a few hours? I couldn't remember exactly. *And how long had I been here?* My mind was racing, taking me to the worst thought of all.

I can't wake up because I'm not asleep.

I looked back at the opening. The mound of dirt blocking my passage was gone, and the exit didn't look that far away any longer. Positioning myself again on my back, I began scooting toward the light. To my relief, I was able to clear the joists. I counted three so far—how many to go? I stopped and looked. Only two more. I was almost to the opening.

Using my arms and legs, I propelled myself as fast as I could toward freedom. The light was getting brighter. Then darkness covered everything, and I hit my head with a crushing blow.

What had I run into? I reached up to feel and realized with horror that it was the drainpipe. How was that possible? It was at the other side. I must have gone in the wrong direction.

Now I was wondering if there were strange gases down here that were making me hallucinate. I had heard of radon gases but thought they only gave off long-term effects. *How absurd to be thinking about radon when I was about to die . . .*

Desperation seized me. I needed to either get out or go insane trying. I could still see the entrance through the dim light and dust. My eyes were burning from the sweat filtering down from my now-completely drenched hair. As fast as I could scoot, I was able to muster up enough energy to move my body toward the entrance once again.

It seemed like an eternity, but right as I was within five or six feet from freedom the dust erupted into my face and momentarily blinded me. Blind as I was, I kept pushing forward and hit my head once again. Seeing stars, I thought, *I must have missed the entrance and hit the wall.* Blinking my crusted, dust-infected eyes, I saw what I had run into. Not a wall but the drainpipe again. *How can this be? Please, God, not again.*

I was almost ready to cry. Was I not being allowed to leave?

Not being able to think clearly in any rational way, it occurred to me that maybe I need to finish the job—the job I'd come here to do. It was worth a try.

What had Carl said? What was I supposed to do? I couldn't think. Then I heard a gravelly voice—not Carl's—whisper, "Angle the drainpipe."

I had to try.

Working my shovel around to the front of me, I slowly moved dirt from under the end of the pipe. I turned the shovel upside down and pushed the loose dirt up to the wall.

My joints were burning now, along with my eyes.

This process was working, and soon the pipe was angling downward. I continued until there was no doubt the pipe was correct, and then I yelled in a voice that was unrecognizable to me, "Never again, Carl!" The task was done—could I now leave this horrible place?

Thoughts of the creepy apparitions rose in my mind. "Where are you? I'm ready for you now! Come and get me now—I dare you."

I looked in front of me. The path to the opening looked as far away as Mars through the dust and dark shadows. It was time to try again.

I quickly scanned the space with my flashlight—no signs of anything. With my upper body propped up on my now-bleeding elbows, I moved forward. My progress was slow but unswerving, until with dust burning my lungs, I went into a violent coughing fit. It soon passed, and so I continued forward, elbows screaming in pain. *Why hadn't I worn a long-sleeved shirt?* I thought.

Then my whole upper body crashed downward into a hole. It was a huge hole where a hole was not supposed to be.

I took a deep breath, collecting myself, and beamed my flashlight around. Now I could see that it was not actually a hole, but a trench, with a path so curved I couldn't see where it was leading. But wait—it seemed to curve back around to where I had come.

Have I gone completely mad? I wondered.

My eyes were borderline useless, but I could vaguely make out the other side of the trench—maybe five feet across. How deep was it? I wasn't sure.

Crawling up to my knees, I looked over the rim. Then a movement caught my eye across the dirt floor to my right.

It was something dark, moving slowly. It was something large.

I blinked rapidly, trying to clear my eyes.

The thing stopped moving.

Then I gasped as the thing slowly rose.

It was a man, yet not a man. The word "monster" was a better description. Part man, part what? Then it came to me, one of the worst of all my childhood fears, and I whispered the name. "Werewolf . . ."

The creature heard me but seemed unaware of my location. Its head turned from side to side in a violent rocking motion. Its snarling jaws were dripping with a dark, thick slime. Large, sharp, sickle-like claws protruded from the sleeves of a scarlet shirt torn to shreds.

Even from a distance, I could feel its breath cryptic and hot, giving off a strong musty smell that reminded me of the gorilla house at the zoo. And from deep in its chest came a low demonic growl.

I saw two evil, red glowing eyes darting back and forth, and its head was slowly moving in my direction. I quickly ducked down below the rim of the trench and retreated away from the monster, trying to stay concealed.

The werewolf's growl echoed throughout the crawl space, making it hard for me to know where it was. But the growl was getting louder.

I focused my eyes down the curve of the trench, expecting him to round the bend. Then the growling stopped. *Was he gone?* I wondered. I crawled forward again. *Had it disappeared just like the green head and the hairy hand?* If so, now was my chance to crawl out of the trench and make my way to freedom. I willed my body to move forward.

Suddenly, the musty smell was back, and I could feel a hot, moist steam hitting the back of my neck. Slowly turning to look upward, I found myself staring into the menacing eyes of the monster.

Not waiting for it to make the first move, I lunged forward, trying to get to my feet but tripped over something in the trench. It was my shovel. Without thinking, I grabbed it and swung back toward the werewolf's head, but he was no longer there. Frantically, I turned back around—there he was. Towering over me, claws out.

His deep growl turned into a high-pitched howl as he leaned his head back and looked to the sky. I also looked up, expecting to see a full moon above like in the old black-and-white movies—but there was no moon, only the bottom of the flooring from above.

With the speed of a cat, he looked back toward me and charged with the rage of an insane bull. I hurled the shovel at the beast as it lunged. The werewolf caught the shovel in its mouth and, using both of its clawed hands, broke it into pieces.

This is it, I thought, *this is the end of my story*.

The wolf was on me, and my world went black.

"Pete!" It was a voice calling me in my dream. "Pete, are you in there?"

Slowly, my conscious mind unfolded. *Where am I?*

I opened my eyes.

I was lying in dirt with my legs straight out in front of me. I remembered the trench, but now it was gone. I then remembered the werewolf and frantically spun my head back and forth—nothing.

"I see you," said the voice. "Are you finished? Come on out. I brought lunch." It was Carl.

I called back to him in a weak voice. "Hold on."

I found I was able to scoot forward toward the opening, which now had a silhouette of Carl on his hands and knees. It only took me a few minutes to reach him.

He pulled me to my feet and told me I looked like crap. Then he handed me a sandwich and a beer. "Did you level the pipe?" he asked.

"Yes, I think so."

I wanted to tell him about what had happened. How I almost died. How I'd seen impossible things. Yet—

How would he believe me? And even if he did, the words of the green head were still ringing in my head, as they would be for years. *"Don't tell anyone, Peter, or I will kill you."*

Carl started up the hill toward his truck, and I followed.

He turned back and said, "Wait, where's my shovel?"

"Yeah, well, it's still way back by the drainpipe, I think."

"No worries," he said, "I'll get it later."

A week later, Carl had me over for dinner. It was Taco Tuesday. My sister, Kate, had all the fixings laid out on the counter and the margaritas were flowing. It was an evening of great food, drinks, and conversation. I hadn't brought up the horrors I experienced while in the crawl space. In fact, the memories of that day were gradually fading, and I wasn't thinking much of them at all—it was better that way.

Carl said, "I have another job for you next weekend, Pete."

"No thanks," I said without hesitation. "I decided I don't need the extra money. I'm just going to pursue some low-cost hobbies like visiting my sister and drinking my brother-in-law's beer for free."

Carl looked slightly bothered at my comment, but still offered me another drink, which I gratefully accepted.

I enjoyed the rest of the evening. I said my goodbyes, gave Kate a hug, and headed down the sidewalk to my car. Carl called down to me as I opened my car door. "Hey, you owe me a new shovel."

"No way, I left it in your crawl space, remember?"

"I know. I went back the next day and found it—found it in about twenty pieces."

My heart skipped a beat.

"Not sure how you could abuse a shovel that badly," he said. "Probably better you aren't working for me anymore." He chuckled as he stepped back inside. "Drive safe—dinner again next Tuesday."

It occurred to me that imaginary wolfmen are not capable of tearing up shovels. *Maybe there are gophers in the crawl space*, I thought.

Then a low howl rose from the distant hills. Startled, I rushed to get into my car, but for some reason, I stopped and looked up into the night sky.

There it was, as bright as the sun itself, a full moon.

Current World

THE VICE HELD THE HOOK in its jaws; the shaft extended out parallel to the coffee table.

A bare hook is the foundation for every fly, a skeletal base in which masterpieces are made. The glare from the shadeless lamp played tricks on the exposed metal, giving this angular snare the look of a vicious snake. Still, the object needed an identity.

His fly box was lacking light-colored nymphs—a proven delicacy for the trout in the South Platte. Luke would remedy this.

He held the jet-black thread against the naked hook, quickly covered it with repeated rotations from the eye to where the hook entered the vice. *Now for the tail*, he thought, as he stripped a few filaments from a duck's down feathers and cinched them to the hook. Just right, not too long, not too short.

Somewhere in the house, a television could be heard. Sounds of an old movie softly echoed throughout the house, rising and falling as the wind outside hit the window. The noises were not a distraction. Sally's voice in his head was a distraction.

The conversation with Sally last night had not gone well. *She had been unreasonable*, he thought. *We'll work it out, we always do.* But now he needed to focus on the fly at hand.

The body of the nymph needed to be formed next. With a small amount of cream-colored rabbit fur, Luke covered one and a half inches of black thread, twisting and pinching until it was in place. The thread now looked like a long piece of moldy spaghetti. Slowly, he wrapped the furry thread around the shaft of the hook, creating a plump but smooth abdomen. He admired his work for a few seconds and sat back in his chair. He then looked over to a framed photo he had sitting at the back of his desk.

"What about the future, Luke?" Sally had asked him. "Does it include me?"

Luke had grabbed a fishing reel from the coffee table while she was talking, which might have been a mistake. *I should apologize for that at least. And I will when she gets back home.*

Luke sat back up and searched through the odds and ends scattered on the table for a small duck feather. He liked to use the tip of these duck feathers for the wings of his nymphs—they looked real, better than most store-bought nymphs for one-fifth the cost. Personal preference played a large part in his creations. He had never taken lessons—he was self-taught.

He placed the base of the feather facing the eye of the hook and cinched it tight with thread. More cream-colored dubbing material was pinched onto the thread and wrapped around to form the thorax. The feathers then had to be split apart with a needle and pulled back before the head of the nymph could be formed. He put the tools down on the desk and sat back in his chair. His mind went back to Sally.

I think I said all the right things, she just doesn't get it, he thought.

"I *am* nothing without you, Sal," he had said. "You are the sun, the moon, and all the tea in China to me." Admittedly, he said it with a bit of playful sarcasm, and while continuing to fiddle with his fishing reel. When he looked up briefly, she was heading to the door. "Wait," he added. "You should come with me."

"I'll pass." She then paused, seeming to wait for a reply from him.

He'd continued to look at his reel, while staying quiet.

"Unbelievable," she said, adding, "I hope you trip on your flippers and go in headfirst."

"I don't wear flippers," he quipped in return, but she was already out the door. He contemplated going after her but decided to wait until she came back. She did not, so he decided to tie flies instead.

I need to focus on this nymph, if it's ever going to get done, he thought. All that was left were the finishing touches. This was Luke's favorite part, and he could perform this step with his eyes shut.

He positioned his whip-finisher and spun it around the eye his usual seven times—no more, no less—to form the head. He pulled the thread taut and clipped it flush with scissors. Leaving the finished nymph in the vise, Luke paused again to admire his work. What a masterpiece it was. He could just picture the trout fighting for the chance to eat his creation.

Sometimes he wondered why he spent so much time making flies that were so perfect. A fish would be fooled by less workmanship, wouldn't they? The fact was, they were a lower level of life and their brains didn't require such artistry. But he enjoyed it. He considered himself a master angler and when he was at the river tomorrow, he would prove it.

Luke glanced at the clock on the far wall—twelve o'clock midnight—time to go to bed and still no sign of Sally.

"It's going to be a wonderful day on the river," he said to no one as he turned off the television and headed down the hall to his bedroom.

The next morning, Luke woke and looked outside—the driveway was empty. *Where could she be?* he thought. He called her on her cell, which went straight to voicemail. "Leave a message," Sally said in a sassy voice.

"Look, I'm sorry," he said into the phone. "I do care about us. Please come home. I'll try harder."

He ended the call.

After some thought, he decided to go fishing anyway. *She doesn't get to ruin all my fun.*

Luke ate a quick breakfast, poured the rest of the coffee into a thermal cup, loaded his truck, and accelerated out of the driveway.

He hurried down the gravel road to the river at a faster speed than normal. Surprisingly, Luke was even more than okay with having to make his own lunch that morning, although Sally usually had it ready for him. It was an unusually calm day on the way to the river. Luke liked calm days—wind and fly fishing were not a great mixture.

His mind was focused on the solitude of the water and the current pressing against his waders. Mostly. Although looking forward to fishing, Luke's thoughts of spending a peaceful day on the water were being overshadowed by thoughts of his troublesome marriage.

The river was Luke's solitude—the place that gave him peace and allowed him to reflect on life. But of course, it wasn't everything. Of course, he wanted Sally to be a part of his life. She would be waiting for him when he got home, and everything would be golden.

As Luke slowed the truck down, pulled over, and came to a stop, it occurred to him that his was the only truck in the parking lot. *Strange,* he thought. There were usually a few cars around, and especially on such a nice day. *Oh well, solitude is why I'm here.*

He got out of the truck, pulled down the tailgate, and started to prepare for the hunt. This portion of the river was considered Gold Medal water, which meant all fish caught had to be released. That's the way he liked it, even though he loved the taste of trout. He preferred to order from restaurants and let others take care of the preparation and the cooking. He fished for sport and not for food.

After his line was rigged with his perfectly tied nymph and the rest of the necessities, he put on his waders and wading boots. Last went on the vest, the vest Sally had gotten him for Christmas. This was where all the flies and cool gadgets he had acquired over the years were stored in an extremely organized manner. Yes, everything was just right and that was important.

"Don't be such a perfectionist," Sally was always telling him. There was a lot of truth to this comment, but he always chose to deny the inference.

With the truck door locked and the key placed securely in the front pocket of his vest, Luke headed down the narrow path to the water, being careful not to make too much noise in the process. Stealth was what came to mind. Approaching stealthily increased one's chances of success.

The cool water pressed against his shins as he entered the current. The water was clear—that was good. When the water was cloudy, fish got spooked, and you might as well go home. Nothing to worry about today.

The fly that he had tied to the end of his tippet was that small, light-colored nymph freshly tied the night before. The water in front of him was the perfect spot for the first cast. With a flip of the wrist, he sent the nymph upriver into the ripple, eddying just below a huge rock. With perfect tension on his line, the strike indicator drifted with the current to lag downstream momentarily. Nothing.

The next cast sent the nymph a fraction closer to the rock—not too much; patience was also a key to success. This time, as the strike indicator floated down, it stopped. Luke lifted his pole up with the necessary force and set the hook.

A fish headed up toward the rock—that was good, better to fight using the current to his advantage than to have the fish head downstream and use the advantage for itself. The battle was over in less than five minutes: the fish was landed, carefully released, and swam away safely to be caught another day.

Luke turned around—a bear was by the shore. Maybe ten feet away and not looking friendly. He carefully backed away into the water, not knowing if this was the best course of action or not. The bear stood up on two legs, and Luke stumbled in surprise.

He fell backward into the stream.

The ice-cold water rushed into his waders, sending shockwaves through his body, and eliminating any chance to regain his footing and avoid the bear, who was now coming toward him. He felt helpless to move—the strong current was pulling him downstream, and the bear was following. When the animal was within striking distance, Luke slipped down into a deep pool and disappeared completely under the water. He remembered thinking, *I didn't know the river was this deep.*

Luke felt completely disoriented, completely submerged in the cold current of the river. However, he was still able to notice how vivid things were. First, he noticed a tiny midge crawling under a rock about ten feet away. Then he saw the rocks and gravel beneath him were teeming with life, and he could see all of it with amazing clarity. He'd never had a view like this. And his body felt different, but in a way hard to describe.

As he watched the river life around him, suddenly a huge paw came crashing down beside him—Luke had completely forgotten about the reason he was in the water—the bear! How could he have forgotten about the bear? Looking up, he could see the animal clearly, in focus without distortion. *Odd*, Luke thought, *having such a clear view while being under the water.* Then the bear's powerful jaws were headed toward him, and without much conscious thought, Luke was suddenly racing through the water with the speed of a missile.

He wanted to stand up and run but could not. Yet still, he was leaving the bear far behind. Luke knew because he was able to see behind him even without turning his head. *That's very strange*, he thought. But he kept going.

When the bear was no longer in view, Luke went behind a large boulder and froze. He felt an urge to stand, but found this simple act impossible. *What's wrong with me?*

He found he could move forward or turn to either direction but could not stand up. Luke tried to put his hand on the creek bed, also with no success. In fact, he was not able to bring his hands in front of his face. Luke's thoughts raced. *Where are my hands? Am I paralyzed? Am I dreaming—am I dead?*

The river had always had a calming effect on him and now was no different. He felt confused but also relatively calm. Being under the water this long in normal circumstances should prove to be deadly, but for whatever reason, Luke was not drowning. In fact, he was breathing—somehow. With the bear out of the picture, he swam like a torpedo toward the surface. His body hit the air with lightning speed, breaking through the top of the water and into the open space above. This venture outside the water was over in a fraction of a second when gravity took over and he came splashing back down.

While breaking the surface, the air had felt strange to his skin. Not bad, but different from what he was used to. It seemed more comfortable in the water than out. *I must have hit my head on a rock and now I'm hallucinating. Or maybe I have hypothermia from the cold water?*

Without really knowing what to do, Luke decided to move around and explore his new world. Keeping an eye out for the bear, he headed down with the current, looking for the spot where he had fallen. Recognizing the area, he stopped and looked around. There was no sign of the animal that had caused his plunge into the water, but something else caught his eye. The familiar item was latched onto a fallen branch in the water downstream. It was his fishing vest. *Now how did that fall off?* he thought.

As he got closer to the vest and swam around to the other side, he was astounded by its size—it was enormous. Then it occurred to him. *Either my vest grew, or I shrank.*

Hanging on the outside of the vest, moving with the current, was a silver lure. Luke moved within inches of the lure and could see a reflection. What he saw was not his face but a wild-eyed trout looking back. Startled, Luke hit the surface, rose completely out of the water, and then came splashing back down once again. He circled back toward the lure. He saw the same reflection, a trout moving as he felt himself moving.

It's me, he thought in shock.

He was looking at a fish in the reflection and the reflection was him—he was now a fish. Now completely sure he was either dreaming or worse, dead, Luke swam around the vest looking for anything at all that made sense. *How can I be a fish? This is not possible.*

He cried out, "Help," but only bubbles escaped his mouth.

"You are really making a lot of noise," a female voice announced.

Luke looked toward the bank. Among the weeds was a rather slender rainbow trout. The lines along her side shone brightly under the sun-filtered water.

"What?" Luke said. He was at a loss.

He understood what she said, not in words but in loud, clear thoughts.

"I said you are making a lot of noise." She swam closer to him.

"I need help," he said, standing his ground, not wanting her to get too close.

"Help? Help doing what?" she answered. With the speed of a missile, she came toward Luke, circled around him, then swam back to a spot in the weeds.

"I'm not supposed to be here," he said.

"Where are you supposed to be?"

Wasn't it obvious? he thought. "I'm not a fish!"

"You look like a fish, a handsome one at that," she said and shyly turned to the side.

"I mean"—Luke tried to gather himself—"for whatever reason, I'm a fish now, but five minutes ago I was a human."

"A human?" She looked confused. "What's a human?"

"A human, you know, not in the water, walking on two legs." Trying to describe a person to a fish was not that easy. "Don't you see things above the water?"

"Oh yes, and I swim away fast!" She demonstrated this by swimming four circles around Luke before he could say his next words. Then she added, "Follow me," as she swam back to the weeds.

Luke didn't follow her but instead went over to the gravel by the shallows of the bank and fell over on his side. He felt like giving up. Then he thought of Sally. *I should have waited for her.* Ironically, he remembered her flipper comment. "I hope you trip on your flippers and go in headfirst."

Had she known? Being too weird to fathom, he put that thought aside. He tried to close his eyes and failed at this simple task. He could feel the life draining from his now-changed body. It was over.

Something pushed him sideways and jolted him back into the current. It was the female trout who had pushed him. "What are you doing?" she asked. "Are you sick?"

"Yes, I think I'm very sick. Isn't it obvious, I mean I'm talking to a fish." He tried to swim back into the shallows, but she cut him off and forced him back, again, into the current.

"Please let me help you—I can help you, but you have to let me." This time Luke stayed with her. He could feel the current of the stream flowing through his mouth and out the side of his head. *Gills,* he thought.

The feeling was relaxing—almost tranquilizing. Soon, he wondered how much time had passed. He had no idea, and really, he didn't care.

The female fish nudged Luke on his side, and this brought him out of the trance. She then turned toward him with what appeared to be a smile on her face. *Are fish capable of smiling?* he wondered. "Let's move to a new spot," she said and darted away upstream. This time Luke followed.

The trip upstream involved quick swimming, then slow, then stopping to explore weedy sections along the bank. It was laid back.

They stopped in a quiet pool below what could have been a beaver dam—it was hard to tell, he had never seen a beaver dam from this angle. The fast water was being blocked by a big log. "We don't want to go up there," the female fish said, pointing her nose in the direction of the larger pool on the other side of the dam. "The big-tailed things make me nervous."

By big-tail things, he assumed she was talking about beavers. "You know, beavers don't eat fish," he said. "They're vegetarians." She just stared at him. "Oh, never mind."

She resumed her swim around the pool, rising periodically to grab insects from the surface. Luke had witnessed this many times when he was fly-fishing—you look for the fish, then place your fly on or under the water for the fish to mistake it for a real insect, and then game on.

"Ah, careful. Ah, Miss Fish, how do you know if that's a real bug or not?"

"Bug? That's a funny name for food," she giggled. "What else would it be?" She immediately darted to the surface for another.

Not knowing how to explain an artificial fly to a fish, he just said, "Just be careful—don't assume everything is food."

"You're funny," she said as she swam around him, then headed to the grasses by the shore.

There were other fish in the pool, all of them rising to eat the dying caddis flies from the surface. Others were nosing along the bottom, eating stone flies that were in the nymph stage. *Wow,* Luke thought. *My fly-fishing knowledge will help me survive this new world.*

Suddenly, Luke was knocked aggressively sideways. After righting himself, he found he was now alongside a much larger rainbow trout. "Are you bothering Misty?" the fish said as he nudged his way even closer.

So Misty's her name, Luke thought. "No, she asked me to follow her."

"Well, you are bothering me. We found this pool first, and therefore this is my food." The big fish violently whipped Luke with his tail, and the pain from the blow shot through his body.

Luke had always been told that fish didn't feel pain, but that thinking went through the window. He saw Misty looking at him from the weeds and quickly swam to her.

"Are you OK?" she said to Luke, as she positioned herself between Luke and the other fish. "Never mind Dart. He's one of my brothers and is extremely rude, some of the time." She glared at Dart, which caused him to swim to the other side of the pool.

"Your name is Misty," Luke said. "That's a beautiful name. My name is Luke."

She giggled and said, "Luke, that's a silly name."

He swam closer to her, then thought, *What are you doing flirting with a fish?* And he thought of Sally. *Not something she would understand.*

Then something caught his eye in the distance outside of the river. It was a person standing in the water near the far bank. *A fly fisherman.*

Having fished this part of the river frequently, Luke knew this pool below the beaver dam. It was a popular spot. He could see the angler holding his line and selecting a fly from his fly box. It was uncanny how clear everything outside the water appeared to him with his new fish eyes.

After a blink, the angler's fly rod was vertical and moving forward, then back. Luke looked at the insects on the surface, looking for the artificial one to appear. Then he noticed Dart, now back in the middle of the pool and looking for food. "No," he yelled to Dart as the artificial fly landed lightly on the water above him.

Dart ignored the warning and headed to the surface, mouth open. He latched on to the fly and took it under. He was immediately rerouted in the opposite direction as the hook was set.

"Swim downstream," Luke instructed, knowing it was harder to land a fish that retreated downstream in fast current.

Dart, being the belligerent fish that he was, again ignored Luke's advice and headed upstream, staying in the pool. Dart fought the tension of the line, crazily surging in multiple directions. He hit the surface, propelling his strong, silvery body into the morning air, recoiling in all directions, and trying to throw the hook from his lip. Dart put up a great fight, but in the end, the fisherman won—Dart, being too tired to fight much longer, was lifted from the water.

"What is happening?" cried Misty. "Where's Dart?"

"It's OK, he'll be back in the water shortly," Luke said. Then, as if on cue, Dart was back in the water with the man's hand holding his body so that water could run through his gills. With a quick flip of his tail, Dart was free. He swiftly torpedoed himself to the nearest cover and disappeared.

Misty looked at Luke with suspicious eyes. "How did you know?"

Luke was surprised she had never witnessed the catch and release of other fish before. She did live in waters where fish were caught all the time. He had always assumed that the fish here were caught multiple times, and after a while, they became suspicious and harder to trick with artificial lures.

"I told you that I was a human and not a fish," he said.

"Help me to understand."

"I'll try, but really, I don't understand either," Luke said. *How could he explain the unexplainable?* "The food Dart just tried to eat was not real. It was made to look real and is tied to a thin line that is used to pull whoever bites it out of the water." He paused—she was clearly trying to understand. "The line is thin, but if you know what to look for, you'll be able to see it."

"And the human who was standing outside the water is on the other side of that line?" Misty said.

"Yes!" Luke had always assumed that trout were incapable of having advanced thought and not able to make rational decisions, but spending the day with Misty was showing this not to be the case.

"I can't believe that you have never witnessed this before. I know this pond is fished regularly. Isn't this your home?"

"Fished!" she said. "Is that what they call this travesty?" Misty swam to the weeds where Dart was hiding. Luke followed. "We don't live here," she said. "We came down from up above just to explore."

They found Dart next to the bank. His eyes were wild with excitement. "That was awesome," he said, still trying to catch his breath.

"What are you talking about? You almost died," Misty said.

"No, the monster let me go," Dart said. "Next time I'll get away before he can grab me."

"No, Dart, there'll be no next time. We need to travel back to our lake. This place is dangerous."

Luke glanced over to where the fisherman was standing. He was gone. *Of course he was gone. After catching a fish, the chances of catching another in the same place were small.* "We're safe for now," he said.

Still excited, Dart said, "I thought the insect looked different, but it just made me mad. What a rush! I want to try again."

"No, Dart. We're going back to our lake."

"Okay," he said. "Maybe tomorrow, I need to rest up." Dart swam back behind the grasses.

"And it was not a monster—it was a human," she yelled. "He's always been difficult," she added, lowering her voice.

"I know the feeling," Luke said, while thinking of Sally. *What's she doing now? Does she even know I'm missing yet?*

They spent the night swimming in the shallow part of the pond. Misty ate various insects crawling along the soft mud that gathered around the rocky riverbed. Luke was hungry but did not relish the thought of eating bugs.

When the morning light filtered its way into the waters of the river, the two swam over to find Dart. He was there, wide awake and looking for food. "Are you ready to swim upstream now?" she asked.

"Not yet—I like it here." He raced away toward the far bank.

"I think you're hopeless," Misty called after him.

Luke turned to watch Dart swim away. There were quite a few trout in the pond this morning, all rising occasionally to eat from the surface. The food was plentiful, but there were still a few scuffles as multiple fish went after the same fly. Then there he was. The first angler of the morning, standing in about the same spot as the one the day before.

As the rod was sent forward, Luke could make out the fly and the line gliding toward the surface of the pond. *Nice cast,* he thought as the fly landed peacefully in the still water above the current.

One of the smaller trout rose to the surface after the fly. Dart came out of nowhere, hit the other trout broadside, then bit the fly himself. He clamped onto it with his jaws and immediately turned downstream into the fast current of the river. The battle lasted only a few seconds as Dart soared into the air a couple of times and spit the fly back in the direction of the angler. He darted from one side of the pond to the next and came to rest beside Misty and Luke. "What a rush!" Dart shouted. His eyes were wild with excitement, and his body was pumped full of adrenaline.

"I don't like this behavior," she said and rammed her nose into Dart's side.

Dart's gills were pumping in and out. "Ouch, settle down, Sis. I'm just trying to have a little fun. It's a rush—you should try it."

"What you're doing is dangerous," Luke intervened.

"Don't be such a minnow," said Dart. "It is not dangerous—I know how to get away now."

"You won't always," Luke said. "You're playing with fire." As soon as the words were out of his mouth, he realized that using fire as a threat to a fish was foolish. The confused Dart stared at him, then swam away.

Luke set out after Misty.

On his way, he looked to see if the angler was still fishing. There was someone standing in the same spot, but this was not the same person—this was a woman. Luke drew closer and saw that it was Sally standing with a hand to her mouth. She was crying. In her other hand, she was holding his fishing vest.

"Sally, I'm down here," he yelled, but she did not hear him.

Another person walked up next to Sally. He was a policeman in full uniform.

Luke tried to listen and realized they were talking about him.

"He always came back home after fishing," she said, and looked down at the vest. "If he drowned, how did his vest come off? It is still zipped up for God's sake."

Luke jumped out of the water, making a big splash. Sally looked down briefly, then looked back to the policeman. "If we could only ask the fish," she said.

"We're looking into all the possibilities," the officer said, "but not that one, however. The facts are that the night park attendant found his abandoned car. No one is allowed in the park after closing. Then he found the vest, hat, and other clothing items. Not knowing what to do next, he called our station." He looked up at the mountain range, then added, "And, of course, there are the fresh bear tracks. But the good news is, there's no evidence of an attack. I'm sure we'll find your husband."

"Is he walking around naked in the hills?" she said. "That is not something Luke would do, ever, I don't think."

"But maybe he's swimming in the river naked!" Luke yelled and jumped with another splash.

The policeman glanced down, thinking to himself that this would be an excellent place to fish. Then he cleared his throat and turned back toward Sally.

"We'll continue to look, ma'am, and you'll get a call if we get any new information."

They both turned and walked out of sight.

Luke yelled again. "Sally, I'm here!" This time he jumped out of the water and onto the shore. *Oh no*, he thought. *I can't breathe*. Luke panicked but was able to flop around until he slid back into the water. He looked back to the ground above the river, but she was gone.

Luke's gills were burning as he tried to recover. He dropped down to the riverbed and remained there contemplating his situation.

"Who was that human?" Misty swam over next to him and rubbed his side with her fin.

"That," he said, still trying to catch his breath, "that was Sally. My wife from another time."

"Wife?" Misty's sad eyes made Luke feel that maybe she understood the concept.

"Yes, you know, like a permanent girlfriend."

"I thought I was your girlfriend?" She waited for a response. When none came, she turned and swam away.

Luke looked back to the shore where Sally had been standing only moments before. Then he turned to watch Misty disappear in the opposite direction. *I was a fool not to go after Sally—am I now making the same mistake?* It was a crazy thought. How could he have a girlfriend who was a fish? His mind was flowing faster than the current.

Luke darted after her. When he caught up, he turned so that their heads were facing. "I said she was from another time. Not this time. Right now, I think I need a friend, and if you still want to be my girlfriend, then . . ." He stopped, not knowing how to finish.

"You can't have two girlfriends," she said, staring at his eyes. "I don't understand how things were in this human world of yours, but down here we're loyal, which means only having one girlfriend. Besides, there are plenty of fish in the river."

Luke laughed at this cliché, then caught himself. "You mean plenty of fish in the sea."

"What's so funny? You're making fun of me because I don't understand your world," she cries. "Well, you don't understand mine either. There are others here in this pond who like me and don't make fun of me. Why don't you go back to your human world and be with that huge, ugly thing you call a wife?"

"First of all, she's not ugly and secondly . . ." He paused and looked to the bank. "Secondly, she can't be my wife anymore because I'm . . . well . . . now I'm a fish. Besides, she doesn't even know I'm still alive." A strange thought crossed his mind. *Maybe I'm not alive, or maybe I'm alive but in a coma.* Putting this thought aside, he continued. "Misty, you're the only part of this bizarre change that is keeping me sane. Please believe me." Then he wondered, *Why did my relationship problems follow me into the river?*

Luke looked back into her eyes. "I know I'm acting strange. It's just that I'm trying to learn a lot of new things right now. I don't expect you to understand, I don't even understand. I don't know what I'm doing here, but I do know one thing . . ." He swam closer. "I want you to be my girlfriend."

Misty's eyes softened. "Then a girlfriend I will be," she said, and swam circles around him, giggling.

If only Sally could have been this understanding, he thought, and started swimming in circles after her.

The next morning, Luke saw darkness outside the water. Clouds covered the sky, and rain was hitting the surface of the river. Huge torrents of water were spilling over the beaver dam and making the river below cloudy. *Probably no anglers will be out today*, Luke thought.

He found Misty feeding on tiny grubs that the current had shaken loose. Dart was there beside her, doing the same. Luke, still not that hungry, said, "Let's visit the beaver pond today. I think we all could stand a change of scenery." *And I won't have to worry about*

Dart and his getting-caught fetish, he thought to himself. "The rain should keep away most of the people fishing."

Misty looked confused, so Luke quickly explained the concept of rain to her.

"I love learning new things," she said. "You're a blessing to me." She then turned and swam away from the dam. "Follow me, Luke!"

Now it was Luke's turn to learn something. Misty turned to face the dam and immediately propelled herself upstream, jumping over rocks and branches. She would disappear for a short moment, then reappear as she continued the ascent. Her last jump took her completely out of the water and into the beaver pond.

Then it was Dart's turn. He used a different path and made it to the pond in half the time. "Try to beat that," he called.

"Don't listen to him, Luke," Misty said. "It's not a race. I know you can do this." She smiled down, and Luke gained some courage.

"Okay—that looked easy. Here I come." His voice sounded more confident than he felt. They made it look easy, but Luke had his doubts.

He took off, trying to follow the same path that Misty took. Somehow, he took a wrong turn and ended up stuck between a couple of branches and suspended out of the water. After a few tries, he was able to wiggle loose, and he found himself back close to where he had started. "I think I've got it figured out now," he said breathlessly. He could hear Dart laughing at him.

The next attempt wasn't much better, but he did manage to get higher before hitting a rock with his head and then sailing back down.

"Come on, silly," Misty said. "You can do this!"

"It is not that hard," Dart said and continued to laugh.

Luke gave himself a few seconds to get his wind and started once more. This time, he was able to keep his speed up, and he sailed over the last cluster of branches into the pond. There, he was greeted affectionately by Misty.

"See, I knew you could." She looked over the few scrapes he had along his side. "You'll be fine." She headed away from the dam. "Okay, guys, let's explore!"

This pond was much larger than the one they had lived in for the last couple of days. Lots of fish swam by to check them out, but they saw them as no threat and let them alone. The beaver house was out close to the middle. However, there were no beavers present. The rain continued to pelt the surface of the water, making it harder to see the outside world.

Unlike most people, Luke had never minded fishing in the rain. He had his best days in the rain. *Maybe because the fish can't see me as well*, he thought.

"How much farther up is your lake?" Luke said. "And how many more beaver dams do we have to pass to get there?"

"The lake is up high, in an area where there are no trees. We took off on our journey when some of the lake was solid and cold. We were in no hurry, and I didn't count the number of nights it took us." She saw the concern on Luke's face. "I do think that going back up will take us longer, and therefore we should start soon." She now looked concerned. "We need to convince Dart to leave too—I won't go without him."

"No, we won't go without him," Luke said, wondering if Dart would be around to make the journey if he continued his "getting caught" addiction.

"The good news is that there's only one more beaver pond in the way."

"Thank goodness," he said.

They continued to watch the other trout in the pond feeding from the mud at the bottom. There were grubs and nymphs in abundance. "I forgot about warning Dart about nymphs," Luke said. "Where is he?" He hadn't seen him since they got to the beaver pond.

"Are they bad? I think they are tasty," she said as she shot down and grabbed one and swallowed it whole.

"Why would you do that when I just told you it was dangerous?" Luke said with a serious stare.

"I saw there was no line hooked to that food. I'm listening to you and want to be safe, but we still must eat. Tell me more about these fake nymphs?" she said, giving Luke her full attention.

"Okay—thank you." Luke could see the dilemma between needing to eat and staying safe. *When was the last time he had eaten?* He couldn't remember. Putting that thought aside, he continued. "When people fish, they sometimes use fake nymphs. I know because that is what I did." Luke thought of the night, not that long ago, when he tied the nymph for this fishing trip. "I'm not proud of this now, but with my knowledge, we can all stay safe." He thought of Dart and how controlling him was difficult. "I'm concerned that if I do tell Dart about this, he'll just see it as another way to have a thrill. And if I don't tell him, he could get caught off guard and panic."

"Tell me what?" Dart said from behind. "What don't you want me to do?"

"Nothing, but I bet I can beat you both to the other side of the pond," Luke said and took off without waiting for a response. About ten feet from the far bank, Misty shot past him like a torpedo. "You're too slow for me," she giggled.

Then Dart shot past, veered upward, and jumped over Misty to win the race. Luke came in last, trying to catch his breath. "You even cheated, and we beat you." Dart laughed.

"I'll get better with practice." He gasped.

Without warning, a huge, brownish animal crashed down into the water between them. "Beaver!" Misty screamed and took off into the deeper part of the pond. The beaver swam after her. "I thought you said the beavers wouldn't bother us?" She zigzagged around the pond with the beast in close pursuit. "Do something! It's going to eat me!"

Dart caught up to the beaver and yelled, "Leave her alone!"

Horrified, Luke stayed where he was, watching, not knowing what, if anything, he could do. He wasn't an expert on beavers and their behavior, but he had heard they were vegetarians. Maybe he had heard wrong.

He took off knowing he had little chance of catching anyone. After all, he had lost the race by a mile, and it was hard to see exactly what was going on because the rain was making the water muddy. He could just make out Misty's silver body with the beaver less than a foot away from her. *Oh no,* he thought, *she's not going to make it.*

Dart shot ahead of the beaver, turned in front of its nose, slapped the beaver with his tail, and swam in the opposite direction. The beaver turned and went after Dart. He was risking his own life for his sister. Then the beaver, after a short chase, turned and went after a different fish, then changed course and went after another. *The Beaver wasn't interested in catching the trout,* Luke thought. It was only taking pleasure in the hunt—the beaver was playing.

He found Misty hiding in the sticks by the dam. She was out of breath and frightened. He nudged up to her and put his fin on hers. "You'll be fine—the beaver was just playing chase."

Dart joined them. "Are you okay, Sis?"

"Yes," she said, "but we should probably get back to our pond."

They all watched as the beaver climbed back onto the bank.

"No rush," Luke said with a smile, "Elvis has left the building."

"Who?" Misty and Dart said in unison.

"Never mind," he said and followed Misty and Dart down through the branches of the dam, over a few waterfalls, and back to the safety of their own pool. Tired from the day's adventure, they settled down next to the grasses along the shoreline and slept.

The next morning, sun filtered down through the vanishing clouds; the rain had stopped; the water was returning to its normal clarity.

The pond was teeming with activity. Fish of all sizes were swimming in their schools. Birds were foraging from the bank along with a small herd of deer that were walking along a sandbar and taking an occasional drink. Insects of all types were abundant. The bigger trout were feeding in the middle of the pond; this included Dart.

Luke spent the morning watching for anglers, who would be more abundant on the weekend. He didn't know what day it was—he had lost track of the days.

Suddenly, something frightened the deer, and they came splashing through the pond just a few feet from Luke. Fish scattered everywhere, trying to avoid being trampled. The deer exited the pond with a couple of leaps and vanished from sight. Luke heard a shriek from behind and turned to see the bear pulling a large trout out of the water with his mouth. The fish cried for help one more time, then went silent. The bear dragged the fish to the shore and slowly ate its meal. Alarmed, Luke went to find Misty. He noticed that the other fish in the pond seemed to be swimming about like nothing had happened.

He found her feeding in the current just below the dam. "Did you see that?" Luke said as he swam down to face her. "How horrible."

"I heard something and swam fast, over here, to get away. What is horrible?" She stopped eating and looked at Luke.

"A bear attacked and ate one of the fish! Didn't you see it? How horrible," Luke said again.

"Oh no! It wasn't Dart, was it?" she said and swam away calling his name.

"No!" Luke answered and went after her.

They found Dart unharmed, which relieved Misty. "You need to be careful around bears. They're not vegetarians and love to eat fish." Then he added, "As many as they can catch."

Luke looked back to the bank. The bear was again going after trout that were trapped between a large boulder and the shore and proved to be easy prey. "Always stay where you have more than one escape route—okay?"

"It is hard to know which monsters chase you for fun and which chase you for food," she answered.

"Good point," he said. "So just swim away from everything and you'll be fine. I just don't know what I'd do if something happened to you."

Misty smiled and moved to Luke's side. "I'll be fine as long as you are my protector," she said, with just a hint of sarcasm.

"Yes, I'll do my best," Luke said with a realization that she, having always been a fish, was better equipped to handle the dangers in this world.

A few days passed, and Dart had not shown any interest in tangling with anglers. "I think he has forgotten about doing that," Misty said. "His memory is horrible most of the time."

"If that's the case, then he'll probably get caught again just by accident." Luke didn't think about trying to lecture him about this danger because it might remind him about the thrill and make him start again. "Maybe now would be a good time to convince him to travel back up to your lake."

"Good idea," she said. "I'll tell him tonight that we will be leaving in the morning after we eat. You'll love it there." Misty got a concerned look on her face. "Do you feel up to the journey? It won't be easy." She looked Luke over. "You have lost weight and strength, I'm afraid. You need to start eating or you'll never make the trip."

Luke didn't deny this. He liked hamburgers and fries, maybe an occasional pizza, but so far couldn't bring himself to eat insects. But he did need to recover his strength. "You're right, Misty. I do need to eat." He looked around at the insects on the surface, then to the ones swimming and crawling on the riverbed. "Which ones do you like the best?"

"Well, let me think," she said, also looking around. "Why don't you try one of these pink ones down here? Follow me."

Luke followed her down and saw what looked like tiny shrimp next to a rock.

"Those are freshwater shrimp!" he yelled. "I love to eat shrimp. I should have thought of this before." Luke remembered that he had quite a few shrimp-looking flies in his fly box.

Not eager to be eaten, the shrimp tried to swim to the safety of the rock. Luke didn't hesitate; he took the shrimp in his mouth and swallowed it whole. *Maybe better with cocktail sauce*, he thought. As satisfying as it was to get food into his belly, there wasn't much taste at all. Still, he swam around the rock, eating them as fast as he could.

"Slow down," Misty warned. "You can't make up for not eating for this long all in one meal. It'll take time to build up your strength. You'll know when you're ready."

Luke spent the rest of the day eating. He forced himself to only eat small amounts at a time. By nightfall, he was trying everything. *Not sure why I thought it gross to eat insects*, he thought. *I am a fish now.*

The next morning, there was a fisherman standing near the shore. He had on full fishing gear; his fishing vest could be seen through his unzipped jacket. On his head was a bright orange bucket hat. He was also holding a small cooler, which he sat down on a flat rock by the edge of the river. As he took off his jacket, he placed it over the top of the cooler. *Must be his lunch*, Luke thought.

The man rigged his line for nymph fishing using one split shot and a bright yellow strike indicator. The fly he chose from his fly box was a small caddis larva nymph, greenish in color. Perfect for this time of year. Luke continued to watch as the man slowly descended into the water on the far side of the river, just down from where the water careened around rocks of various sizes.

Luke felt confident that he had educated Misty well as to what to look for to tell a real insect from its fake counterpart. Also, he had last seen Dart in the weeds behind, nowhere near the fisherman. They should be safe.

Luke stayed still in the still water of the pond and watched. The angler's casts were smooth, sending the fly up into the faster water and letting it drift down below. On the third cast, a rather large trout was fooled and took the fly. Luke was not too concerned, knowing that the rules of the river were to release all fish unharmed.

The man took the net that was hooked to the back of his vest and scooped the fish from the water. He reached into the net and pulled the fly from the trout's lip. Then he got up and carried the trout inside the net over to the cooler. He opened the lid and slid the failing fish inside. *He was a poacher.*

Luke watched with horror.

"You can't do that," he shouted as he stuck his head above the water. "This is Gold Medal water!" The fisherman paid him no mind. The man then walked downstream, where he began casting his line again, until he landed another fish and once again deposited it into the cooler.

After Luke witnessed another three fish find their way into the cooler, the man gathered his belongings and walked away out of sight.

Luke searched for Misty and found her near the waterfall playing in the current. "We have a problem," he said. "One of the anglers is taking his catch and not letting them go."

"Oh no. What will happen to them?" she asks.

Luke knew what would happen to them, but just said, "We'll never see them again."

"We must tell Dart," she said, and turned to swim away.

"Hold on—we have time for that later."

Misty stopped and circled back.

"The fisherman has gone for now, and as far as I know, he may not return. However, I'll recognize him if he does. He was wearing a bright orange hat. Easy to spot." *I know he'll be back. You always go back to where you catch fish,* he thought. *Hopefully, when he does return, he will be wearing the same orange hat.* "My strength is coming back. I can feel it. I think that after two more nights I'll be ready for the trip upstream."

"How exciting! I'll prepare Dart for the trip. I know how he hates surprises." She hurried away to find him.

Luke was relieved that they had a plan. His job, for the moment, would be to regain his strength.

He spent the remainder of the morning feeding both from the riverbed and from the surface. His thoughts drifted to Sally. "I guess this is truly goodbye, my love," he whispered. If she ever came back to the bank, he would not be there.

He swam to the shade of the grasses by the bank and thought of her. *She will spend the rest of her life wondering what happened.* This filled him with sorrow. *I hope she doesn't blame herself.*

He tried envisioning her face but found some of the details were fading. *I can't let this happen. I must think of her more often.* Depression crept in, and he found that the more he tried to imagine Sally's face, the more of it he couldn't remember.

Then he thought of Misty and his new life. This eased the pain, slightly. Not wanting the depression to get the best of him, he forced himself to continue eating. This too helped, but not much.

The day was long, but eventually the sun disappeared behind the mountain range, signaling the end of another day. Luke continued feeding throughout the night; the moon was full, and the insects were abundant. After a while, Misty joined him, and all thoughts of Sally were gone.

The next day brought a few anglers, none of whom were wearing orange hats. A few fish were caught, and all were released, unharmed. Sally had prepared Dart for the journey. They would be leaving in two days. All fears of Dart not wanting to go were gone. He seemed anxious to get back to his home lake and see his friends and family again.

As a fish, preparation for a trip was not difficult. There was nothing to pack and, of course, no car to prepare. One more day of eating to gain his strength was all Luke needed. He felt like he was already fit enough, but Misty persuaded him to follow the schedule. There was no rush.

"I can't wait for you to meet my other brothers and sister," she said the next morning as they circled in and out of the faster current, pausing only to grab a snack from the mud. "You won't believe how clear and cool the water is."

Luke only smiled at her, thinking that he did know these things based on a few trips to the lakes above the timberline.

"I've made a few other friends in this pond and a few of them will be swimming up with us," she said. "I hope you're okay with this."

"Of course, I think that's a great idea," he answered, but wondered if safety in numbers applied to fish.

Luke swam to a calm section of water by a sandbar. Misty followed him and nuzzled up to his side. "Misty, I want you to know that I'm excited about my new life, mostly because I'll be spending this new life with you. I think you've been the missing part in life all along." She pressed harder against his side and giggled. They both thought traveling day couldn't come soon enough.

The full moon shone bright again that night, and they stayed snuggled side by side.

Daybreak brought life to the pond. Deer were drinking from the bank. The beaver was crawling along, inspecting his dam and making a few adjustments.

Misty had left earlier to find Dart to make sure he was still onboard for the next day's journey, and Luke was feeding from the surface in the deepest part of the pond.

He didn't notice when a chubby raccoon raced across a fallen log and scampered away. Or when the beaver dove into the pond out of sight, and the deer raised their heads, turned, and bolted off to the safety of the forest.

Luke continued to feed, oblivious to the commotion outside of the water. His mind was elsewhere, thinking about the journey ahead with unknown dangers and challenges. He would have to trust Misty and Dart and their knowledge of the terrain.

A sudden commotion below the pond brought Luke from his daydreaming state. He turned to look. About one hundred yards downriver was the man with the orange bucket hat, and he was in the process of landing a large trout. After successfully landing his catch, he walked over to his cooler, removed the jacket covering it, and slid the fish inside. Luke was not surprised: he had expected the man to return but hoped it would be after they left the pond.

Luke continued to watch. After a few unsuccessful casts, the orange hat guy gathered his things and walked upstream toward Luke.

I need to find Misty and Dart, he thought, and swam around aimlessly. When Luke looked back, the guy was standing just across the pond. His jacket-covered cooler was on the rock, and he was rerigging his line, changing from nymphs to dry flies, and why not, the pool was teeming with rising fish. The man descended the bank and stepped into the water, stripping out line from his reel as he went. Luke still could not find Misty and Dart.

The poacher's first cast was successful, but only for a moment, as the fish who took the fly was able to release the hook with one quick flash of its tail. Luke was getting more stressed out by the second. "Everyone, stop feeding!" he yelled. A few of the fish looked his way, considering what he had said, then went back to what they were doing.

The second cast sailed to the middle above the deepest part of the pool. Immediately, a younger trout raced to bite the fly. Out of nowhere, swimming from the boulders on the riverbed, shot Dart. "No, Dart, it's a trap," Luke called.

Ignoring the warning, Dart continued toward the fly. His mouth was open wide, inches from his prize, when another fish came out of nowhere and hit him broadside. They both went sailing out of the water. Dart swam away in disgust, but the other fish was hooked, not in the mouth but snagged along its side. "Foul caught" was the term for this illegal way of catching fish, but this knowledge was the furthest thing from Luke's mind as he froze with shock.

The fish that hit Dart, who was now fighting for its life, was Misty. Luke watched in horror as she streaked to one side of the pond and then to the other in an attempt to shed the hook. He raced toward her with the hope of somehow helping her free herself. *I need to bite through the line*, he thought, but through all the white water from the splashing, he couldn't find it.

Misty fought gallantly, but soon exhaustion took over, and she was pulled within striking distance of the net. She made one final attempt and came out of the water, startling the man, and making him stumble backward. Then Luke saw the line gleaming in the sunlight. He soared into the air, mouth open, and bit it. Misty was free, but disoriented, and she swam toward the bank of the river and not to the safety of the open water. The orange hat guy scooped her up in one quick motion. She was in his net, and Luke watched in terror as he ascended the bank and headed to his cooler.

Luke saw red. His heart was beating so hard it shook the ground. "No!" he screamed at the top of his lungs. *I can't let this happen.*

Luke tried to jump out of the water, but the current held him back, and besides, what good would that do? Man against fish. Then suddenly the water became bitterly cold. The once-gentle current changed into a raging cyclone. The strong current surged about his body. The river continued to spin in a circular motion. He had to get to Misty; he was her protector.

Anger continued to swell inside him, and his strength increased.

On the shore, the man put Misty into the cooler. He then proceeded to walk along the riverbank heading to the pond.

Luke's strength amplified, and he was able to control his body within the current, the river still swirling around his body. He brought his head out of the water and could see the cooler and the orange bucket hat as it ascended over the upper beaver dam. The water stung his eyes as he turned his head upward to the sky.

Luke rose from the water.

He did not stop until he was completely upright, standing on two feet. He looked down at his naked body, now covered with mud, not a fish but a human. Luke stepped up onto the land and walked over to the cooler. Inside were two fish, one in not too good of shape but still alive, and there was Misty. She was trying to catch her breath.

He picked her up.

She looked him in the eye, recognition descending immediately.

Luke grabbed the other fish and tossed it quickly into the river, hoping it would survive. Knowing the proper way to release a fish, he carried Misty down the bank and held her so that the water was moving through her mouth and gills. In an instant, she twitched her body with a powerful force and left his hand. She was gone. Luke felt a combination of gratitude and sorrow. "Goodbye for now, Misty," he said, then turned to look for the poacher.

Luke could see the top of the orange hat just peering over the gnarled branches and logs of the upper beaver dam. He picked up the guy's jacket and wrapped it around his waist, then proceeded to climb the bank up to the second beaver pond.

The guy was in the process of tying on a different fly. He looked up just as Luke cleared the last branch of the dam. "This is my spot, dude," he said and looked back down at the fly in his hand. Then, realizing what he had just seen, he slowly looked back.

Luke was soaked, his body a tangle of weeds and mud. His face was contorted into a snarl with his teeth showing. He looked like a deranged zombie.

Without stopping, Luke leaned down and grabbed a stick the size of a baseball bat. "I'm going to teach you a lesson about poaching," he said in an angry voice that even he didn't recognize.

The guy dropped his fly rod and backed away. "Hey, you're the dude on the posters—the one missing," he said, looking around for an escape route.

"No, I'm the dude that's going to crack your head open. These are Gold Medal waters, and all fish must be released—*unharmed*." As Luke spoke the last word, he raised his club to strike. The poacher avoided the blow, jumped over a log, and ran off into the protection of the trees. "Go away," he yelled back. "I didn't do anything."

Realizing that he would not be able to catch him being barefoot, Luke watched the orange bucket hat disappear into the forest. He tossed the stick into the weeds, tightened the jacket around his waist, and walked down the embankment to look for Misty.

It was a beautiful day, the bright sun filtering down through the tall Ponderosas to create shadows on the surface of the water. The sound of the water, loud and pouring down from above, mingled with the sounds of birds. He could only think of one fish.

Luke walked and found the place where he exited the river and sat down on a boulder, resting his bare feet on the riverbed. The coolness of the water as the current rushed through his toes was refreshing.

"I'm sorry, Misty," he said, "I can't be with you now. You'll have to make the journey without me. Take care of Dart and take care of you." Luke looks into the sky. "I miss you so much already."

Something rubbed against his toes, and he looked down to see a rainbow trout lying in the pebbles by his feet. It was Misty.

She swam upward; her head broke the surface. Luke saw her mouth moving, but he was unable to hear anything. She backed down into the water, rubbed slowly against the side of his foot, and with a flash of her tail, disappeared into her world within the current.

Luke continued to sit on the rock. He had no way of telling how long. He was thinking of Misty.

Then suddenly, Sally's face appeared in his mind, her smiling face with all the details that had vanished. "Sally," he whispered. He got up, looking around for the trail that would lead him back to the parking lot. He adjusted the jacket again to keep it from falling off and then noticed something in the pocket. It was the guy's wallet with his driver's license. *I guess you will get to pay for your crimes after all*, he thought, and walked down the trail away from the river.

After the initial shock of having her husband found naked, wrapped in someone else's jacket, Sally was able to accept Luke's explanation of "I can't remember anything after the bear chased me into the water." She still had lots of questions but let them go because she was happy he was alive—and happy with his new attitude. She found him more caring toward her, more wanting to spend time together as a couple. Also, they agreed that going to marriage counselling would be a good thing.

The day after he had been found, two weeks from when he disappeared, Luke had turned the jacket over to the game warden, with the wallet and a detailed explanation about what the jacket's owner had done. It turned out that orange bucket hat's name was Kyle Turner, and he didn't have a fishing license, therefore should not have been fishing. However, there was no proof of Luke's allegations, and the guy claimed he was not fishing, just hiking by the river. The cooler was found—it was empty, of course. Kyle Turner was released without penalty.

"He got off easy," Luke said one night as he and Sally were enjoying one of her famous homemade lasagnas. "I mean, those poor fish and the suffering they went through."

"How do you know fish suffer? They are just stupid fish," she said as she waved away a house fly circling her lasagna. "You like to eat fish—don't be such a hypocrite."

"First of all, they are not stupid, and don't you think that it would also hurt to have a hook in your mouth, and then be pulled out of the water?" he said, sipping his wine and looking at the fly that had now landed on Sally's shoulder. She flicked it away. "That's why I'm selling all my fishing gear and buying a camera."

Sally's mouth dropped open in disbelief.

"This way I can still enjoy going to the river to take pictures and not to torture fish." The fly landed on the table next to Luke's plate. He watched it for a second, then looked back at Sally. "Maybe you could go with me; it will be fun; we'll take a picnic lunch."

"Yes, I think I'd like that," she said, smiling, as Luke slapped his hand down and killed the fly. "Nice shot," she said. "Now clean up that mess."

Luke grabbed the fly, held it up to his face, popped it into his mouth, and swallowed it down.

Sally looked on in horror as Luke got up from the table, walked to the sink, and washed his hands. "Oh, honey, what happened to you up there?"

"I really don't remember," he answered.

Luke sat back down to eat his lasagna.

Sally said something else, but Luke did not hear her. His mind had returned to the currents under the river and to thoughts of Misty.

The Drum Tech

THE VAMPIRE DANNY BARROW walked the streets of Chicago alone. Not that there were no others like him, but somehow, he just didn't fit in—in any part of the world. Danny liked to travel, mostly within the United States. He got his fill of the European countries years ago and was able to stowaway on a luxury cruise ship to cross the Atlantic. He imagined that someday he might go back, but with so much time on his hands, he was in no hurry.

Wherever he lived, he was able to hire a loyal non-vampire, or what in the vampire world is called a familiar. Robert was his latest and had been working for Danny for about six months, since he first arrived in Chicago. Robert didn't talk a lot, but what he lacked as a conversationalist, he made up for with his loyalty and service. For one, Danny was unable to operate a cell phone. His fingers didn't register on the touch pad, making the device useless. If something needed to be done by cell, Robert had to do it. Mostly, Robert was a big help doing things for him during the day. During the night, it was Danny's time to feed. He lived mostly on wild animals but not entirely—he was a vampire after all, and sometimes he couldn't resist the taste of human blood. Not much different from non-vampires not resisting a nice juicy steak.

And sometimes, he needed a little extra something. Boredom was commonplace for Danny and had been for hundreds of years.

For one thing, Danny found that finding female companionship was difficult. The differences between a human and a vampire are light-years greater than any generational gap. Then there was the fact that if a vampire is careful, they can live forever, and consequently, if not converted, a human will age and then die—a relationship killer for sure. Yet, even though all his relationships ended poorly, he never gave up.

Mostly, Danny lived with the boredom, but being a predator, he loved the thrill of the hunt, which he pursued in various forms. Music also gave him a release from tedium, and he attended many concerts at night. He could always get in without a ticket—no one ever asked him.

One of the bands he liked had just acquired a new lead guitar player, who caught his eye while he was reading a music tabloid he came upon next to a dumpster outside an abandoned warehouse. Her name was Sonya, and she had the look that Danny was drawn toward. Her eyes seemed to call to him in a way that, if he had breath, would have taken it away. And she had the appearance of someone who would consider joining the ranks of the vampire nation. Still, it was only some pictures in a magazine. He needed to see her in person and hear her play.

Since he was more of a doer than a wisher, pursuing this guitarist was already in the planning stages.

The article included the tour dates. Danny skimmed the list, his eyes quickly finding Chicago. *That's lucky*, he thought. The hard part would be getting her to like him without the use of mind control. For even though he was a vampire, he was a true romantic.

Danny set the tabloid aside, looked up into the night sky, and flew away in the form of a bat.

"This never gets old, does it?" asked Wolf Mixon as he poured himself another gin and tonic at the hotel wet bar. "Matt? Sonya?"

"Sure, but I'll take a beer," said Matt, walking over to the small refrigerator to help himself. He taped out a rhythmical beat on the top of the fridge before opening the door. "Living the dream never gets old."

"Sonya?" Wolf asked again.

Sonya looked up from the guitar magazine. "Oh, no thanks, I've had enough," she answered and then went back to the article, which was introducing the latest fashion in guitar straps. She thought it was interesting, even though all her straps were custom made. *Maybe I'll go with greens and purples for the next tour*, she said to herself.

The Wolf Mixon Band was forty years in the making and still going strong. In part because Wolf surrounded himself with talent and good looks. In Wolf's opinion, the success of a band was in making sure everyone attending saw not only a concert, but a show. The show needed to be amazing, not only for the ears but also for the eyes.

His loyal fans loved him and marveled at his ability to stay young both in spirit and appearance. He attributed this to the overall youth of his band members, working out in the gym, and always using the best makeup money could buy. He had managed to keep his health, which, in turn, helped keep the concert schedule going.

All bands have their secrets, and The Wolf Mixon had their share—these secrets were kept close to the cuff.

"When was Reed getting back?" asked Sonja, looking up from the magazine. Reed Collins was the bassist.

Wolf shrugged his shoulders—some secrets were even kept from the rest of the band members. "Don't worry about Reed," Wolf finally answered. "He can take care of himself. He'll be at breakfast in the morning. I have no doubt."

"Okay then. On that note, I think I'll see you two in the morning at breakfast. With Reed." Matt chuckled, grabbed another beer, and headed to the door.

"Me too," Sonya said, hugging Wolf before following Matt, taking the magazine with her.

"Breakfast at eight, then we'll check out the venue," said Wolf as the door closed. "Don't be late," he said to himself, and refreshed his drink.

The band put out a new album yearly, in which none of the songs made the Top 40 anymore; a curse for all bands associated with the classic rock genre. Still, he was managing to keep the older fan base, along with many of the younger, mostly goth, generation, coming to his concerts. The new songs never made the show, but were played while the guests were entering the concert hall.

Wolf, the only original member of the band, prided himself as a showman with lots of props and shocking dramatics to go along with his hits from the past. The stage crew and the guitar and drum techs were always the first to arrive, giving themselves ample time to set up the elaborate stage. Over the years, it had grown to quite a sight, with towering cathedral walls with roof lines equipped with menacing gargoyles, and lifelike bats and spiders—a real Halloween show.

Having top-notch crew members was the key to performance success. Everything had to be timed out perfectly, theatrics along with the pyrotechnics. The crew members were up to date on their knowledge and always pushed the limits.

Each venue was different, and quick modifications were needed to make everything look and sound amazing. The numerous guitar techs had been on Wolf's crew for decades and were considered the best in the business. Thurston was the head of the stage crew, and he was the one you wanted to be in charge when excellence was a requirement. Everyone had their specialty with lots of backups in all the areas. However, there was only one drum tech—his name was Phil.

Phil made every drum kit used along the tour sound awesome, regardless of make and model. If any function of the drum kit malfunctioned during a performance, Phil was quick on the scene, dressed all in black, to remediate the problem without missing a beat—so to speak.

It was late July, and the United States tour was a little more than a third over—the band and their crew had been working together as one seamless unit for months.

Next on the schedule was the Huntington Bank Pavilion in Chicago. It had been sold out for weeks.

Sonya's room was on the next floor above Wolf's suite. She never got a suite but didn't care, since she had no intention of entertaining.

Matt had gone down the stairs to his room, so she was taking the elevator alone, up to her floor. Sonya wondered why their agent always booked all the band members' rooms on different floors and made sure each floor they were on was off limits to other guests. It seemed like a waste of money. *That's what you get when you leave men in charge*, she thought.

The elevator stopped, and the doors opened. Sonya stepped out and began walking toward her room. Then she saw a dark figure at the end of the hall, and her heart skipped a beat. She stopped. It was a man dressed in all black, in what appeared to be a tux. He was strikingly handsome with a well-kept five o'clock shadow and dark, piercing eyes.

Sonya called to him, "I don't think you are supposed to be here."

The man pointed to something behind her. She looked to see what it was and then immediately turned back.

He was gone.

"Where did you go?" she called to the man who was no longer there. "It's fine, I won't tell."

It did bother her that he seemed to just disappear. *Maybe he just went into one of the other rooms*, she thought. But they were supposed to all be empty. "Sonya, maybe you had one too many drinks tonight," she said quietly to herself and walked over to her door.

She reached into her back pocket and pulled out the keycard. When she went to press it to the door's touch pad, it slipped from her fingers and fell to the ground. With a quick glance down, she snapped her fingers. The card flew back into her hands, and she again lifted it to the door's touch pad. The light turned green, and she went inside.

Everything was quiet. She shut the door behind her and walked around the room, opening the closet and the bathroom doors—nothing. She took a deep breath and went into the bathroom to prepare for bed. Her powers allowed her to do simple tasks like retrieve a card from the floor, turn on lights, and turn down the covers of the bed. She kept this to herself. Her mom had similar powers and taught her to use them cautiously. "You control the power and never let it control you," her mother would tell her.

Once, when she was about twelve years old, Sonya was playing chase with their dog, Riggs. She accidentally kicked the ball over the wooden security fence. Then she screamed and yelled, "I hate you!" The fence exploded—boards went everywhere, barely missing her and Riggs. She walked through the hole where the fence had once been to get her ball.

Her mother, watching from the window, ran outside, grabbed Sonya, and took her in, where she received the scolding of her young life. "Do you realize the consequences of your actions, young girl?" There was more, but that was what she remembered from the incident. And that her dad was also angry. Mostly because he then had a fence to repair. Sonya knew she could do lots of damage with her powers, and over the years, she became able to handle her anger in other ways.

As she lay in bed, she put no thought to her unusual powers, but instead thought of the mysterious man in the hallway and his seeming powers. *How had he been able to just disappear?* she wondered.

Danny made his way through the jam-packed crowd, not drawing attention of any kind, blending in with everyone else. He loved Chicago because he could always blend in. Most big cities were like this. And this venue was dark, on the edge of goth. All forms of darkness were the best cover for his kind.

He was able to get in, as always, to the venue. No one asked him for a ticket. It was a mind game he had learned and was now quite good at—having people do what he wanted.

Inside the concert pavilion, the live music had already started—it was loud and edgy, the way he liked it. His destination was to be as close to the stage as possible. Making his way there was easy—everyone just got out of his way, no confrontation needed.

Reaching his destination and looking up at the stage, there she was, the one he came here to see. *There must be a way to get closer,* he thought. He walked up and stood next to the bouncer on the side of the stage.

Danny reached out and touched the stage. The bouncer gave him zero notice.

There she was again, only about ten feet from him and even more beautiful than she had been in the hallway the other night. Now she was midway through the solo break of one of the band's more famous songs. Narrowing his eyes, he concentrated on her thoughts. She stumbled; her guitar let out a loud, off-key squeal. Another guitar player noticed and covered for her.

She turned toward him, and their eyes linked for a few seconds. Then he turned away and released her. She shook her head and went back to playing. When she turned back to look at the mysterious figure, he was gone. She remembered the man in black who had startled her in the hallway. *Same guy?* she thought. *Maybe.*

Danny maneuvered around to the side of the stage. *Darn,* he thought. *She recognized me from the hotel.* He didn't want her to think of him as some creepy stalker.

Being this close to the stage, he noticed lots of commotion going on behind the scenes—people running around grabbing guitars, moving cables, changing mics, and then there was the one guy who was adjusting a cymbal stand that had come loose. "Well," he said softly. "That's a job I could do." He studied what the guy was doing. Mostly just hanging out at the back of the stage, in the dark. *My kind of job*, he thought.

Danny slipped silently further along to the back of the stage, still going unnoticed. He was as stealthy as an alley cat stalking mice. When he brought his eyes up just above the level of the stage, there he was, the drum adjuster guy, dressed all in black. *Yeah, just like me.* Patiently, Danny waited to make his move. He lived for this kind of cat-and-mouse game; that is, if he would have been alive.

Phil, having corrected the angle of the main crash cymbal, sat quietly watching the drum kit. He could always tell when something was wrong, sometimes even before it went wrong. *Good so far*, he thought. Something drew his attention to his left. The something was rolling toward him.

Phil reached into his pocket and drew out his pen light, turned it on, and aimed at the thing rolling toward him. It was small and black, kind of furry. Unfamiliar. It stopped about six feet from him. Then, two wings opened to the sides and a rat head came up slowly. Its eyes were dark and piercing, like the eyes of a doll. *It must be some sort of stage prop that got away from someone,* he thought. But then the bat thing grew to the size of a large dog.

Phil was paralyzed in fear.

The thing's mouth was opening and shutting, but it was the eyes that drew him in. Phil was unable to turn away—he didn't want to turn away. A voice came into his head.

"You are being relieved of your duties. You must quit." Along with the words, horrible visions popped into his head. Then the voice roared, "NOW!"

Phil jumped back, almost falling off the back of the stage.

His mind was altered in such a way that staying was not an option. He needed to get away. He needed to leave or something bad was going to happen. He had no idea what the bad thing was because the thing was beyond imaginable. The will to leave was only outweighed by the need to inform Thurston, the head stage manager, who was just coming out of the backstage exit. He stumbled over to him.

"What's the matter, Phil? You look like crap."

Phil just stared for a few seconds, then said, "I quit, man, find someone else," and ran for the backstage door.

"Come on, Phil, this is no time to . . ." Thurston's voice trailed off as his reliable drum tech disappeared out of sight. He stood looking at the exit with his mouth wide open.

One of the guitar techs came up to him. "What was that all about?"

"Not sure. Phil just quit—bad timing on his part. Maybe you could go and run him down."

"Okay, boss," he said and ran through the exit door.

Having been in the business for going on forty years, Thurston had seen it all, but still this caught him off guard. But for only a moment.

He didn't have time for selfish HR problems, and besides, all that mattered now was ensuring a successful concert. He would deal with Phil later.

He didn't notice the bat flutter by his head and dive down beside the stage. But he did notice the dark figure that suddenly appeared behind him. The man said, "Hello, I think I'll be able to help you with this situation."

"What? Huh? What situation?" Thurston regained his wits. "Who are you and what are you doing back here?" Normally, he would have called for security, but for some strange reason, he felt no need. In fact, he wanted to hear what this strange man had to say. "How can you help me?" he asked.

"Well, I noticed the man who takes after the drums walked off the job. How unfortunate—and right in the middle of a concert." The man stepped forward out of the shadows.

"Yes, our drum tech quit for some reason," Thurstan said, looking the man over from head to toe. He was well dressed, totally in black. His eyes were the strangest part—dark as coal. "Unless you know a drum tech, who's here in this room right now, then you can't help me."

"Drum tech? Yes, I'm a professional drum tech," Danny lied. "You'd be hard pressed to find anyone better, even if it weren't at such short notice. This is your lucky day." His voice was smooth with a slight accent that Thurston couldn't distinguish.

"I didn't catch your name," Thurston said.

"My name's Danny Barrow," Danny responded with a slight bow. "And yours?"

"It's Thurston." He paused. "How long have you worked as a drum tech? Who have you worked for?"

"That is not any concern of yours, Mr. Thurston." Danny's stare intensified.

"I suppose not," the man said, backing away slightly. "And it's just Thurston. Can you start now?" The words were coming out of his mouth, but he couldn't believe what he was saying. He was always strict with his hiring, checking all qualifications and talking to all references. But now he was hiring this guy without knowing anything about him. *Maybe I'm just desperate*, he thought.

"I can," Danny said, and in one leap, he jumped onto the stage and moved quickly to the drum kit like a cougar pouncing.

Matt was keeping a steady beat to the song that was playing, when something caught his eye. Then it was gone, then back again. "What the hell?" he said.

Danny was going around the drum kit, tightening wing nuts at a pace Matt was not used to seeing. Matt looked around for Phil, who was nowhere to be found. He had no choice but to ignore this new drum tech and turn his concentration back to the rhythm of the song.

When Danny had finished tightening everything, he looked over at Sonya. She was staring at him, openmouthed.

He gave her a quick wave and winked, then fled to the back of the stage out of sight. Sonya raised her hand to wave, then stopped and went back to the guitar.

Danny had adjusted everything on the drum kit in record time and had done it so well that there were no more issues for the rest of the show. He was a very fast learner and seldom made mistakes. Being a vampire did have its benefits.

This job did too.

Before he leapt to the back of the stage, he'd looked back at the drums. In a flash, he admired not only their sound, but the craftsmanship used for their construction. He couldn't imagine a more beautiful sight. *I will enjoy this*, he thought.

At the end of the concert, Danny introduced himself to Matt and proceeded to dismantle the drum kit. It was a no-brainer as each piece had its own case. Then he took everything out the back exit and stacked each piece carefully into the semitruck that was backed into the loading dock. Sonya had disappeared at the end of the show. He had hoped to at least introduce himself to her as well.

Thurston was standing outside of the exit and waved Danny over. "Hell of a job, son," he said and handed him a piece of paper.

Danny examined the paper, which read "contract" at the top. "Contract?" he asked, still staring down at it.

"Yes, fill this out and bring it back with you tomorrow morning when we're finishing up."

"I'll fill it out now. May I borrow a pen?" he asked.

"Sure, here you go," Thurston said and handed him a pen that was in his shirt pocket. "No hurry, tomorrow will be fine."

Danny took the pen over to a small table at the corner of the stage and returned a few seconds later. He handed the contract back to Thurston. "Here you go—I only work at night."

"That won't work," Thurston said.

"Yes, it will," Danny told him.

"Okay, that'll be fine. Only at night. No problem," Thurston replied, but had no idea why.

"I'll meet you in St. Louis in two days," Danny said, remembering the concert schedule.

"Yes, St. Louis, right." Thurston was in a daze. "We start set up in the morning. But how will that work if you only work at night?

"The drum kit will be ready," he said, then added, "Trust me." Danny made a slight bow and exited the backstage area with the speed and grace of a cat.

Thurston blinked his eyes, then looked down at the contract. Everything looked complete. Although, it puzzled him how extraordinary the penmanship was, having been filled out so quickly. He shrugged his shoulders, folded up the contract, and put it back into his pocket, not noticing that his pen was not returned.

Danny made his way back to the alley, which was two blocks from Sonya's hotel. Trying to see her again would be risky—he could seem like a real night stalker—so he decided to just see her at the next gig in St. Louis. Now his only thought would be to arrange travel plans to the city with the big arch. He could fly as a bat, although he might not be able to make it before the sun came up. What he needed was his own car. One big enough to transport his casket and other belongings—which he had few—he did now have a pen. When he got back to the house, he would have Robert look online to find a suitable car or truck.

On the way home, he saw a copy of a small local newspaper that had been discarded and was about to be sucked down into a sewage drain. He remembered when the newspaper was a good place to find listings for used cars, but nowadays, everyone was shopping online. He flipped through the soggy paper with not much hope of finding anything, and was just about to throw the paper back into the gutter, when he came across a section entitled, "Classifieds." It was only one page, but did include a few automobiles for sale. He used the pen to circle all the possible vehicles that would meet his needs—there weren't many. There was a 2010 Yukon, and a 2007 Suburban, both of which were possibilities, and both could already have been sold. The Suburban would probably work the best, but it would still be a struggle to get a heavy casket into the back. Then he noticed a small section at the very bottom of the page that was labeled "Novelties." The listing read: *For Sale: Late model Cadillac Hearse. White, Good condition, $45,000, firm.* "Perfect," he whispered. It would be like a camper for vampires. He would have Robert check to see if it was still available and would send him tomorrow to make the purchase. He realized that it would have to be a cash offer; he needed a clean title. Danny had plenty of cash saved up over the years. His only concern was that he didn't know if Robert had a driver's license. No big deal if he didn't, but a huge deal if he couldn't drive. Excited to get home quickly, he flew the rest of the way as a bat, with the classified section of the newspaper flapping, clutched in his claws.

The hearse, at least online, was still available, and greatly reduced from the listing in the paper.

"We're going to do a lot of traveling in the next few years. Can you drive?"

"Yeah," Robert muttered.

"Very good," Danny said and sat down beside him to go over the details for the next day.

Robert would be on his own to acquire the hearse and the necessary paperwork to make it legal. He didn't question any of the tasks he would have to do. Danny knew he wouldn't.

After wishing him good luck, Danny went to the back bedroom, opened the casket, and brought the lid down on top of him. The darkness was very comforting, and he fell asleep thinking of Sonya—his plan was coming together.

When Danny crawled out of his casket at sunset, he found the hearse parked outside. It wasn't in great condition, but he figured it must at least run. When he opened the back hatch to find a roller system that was made to accommodate a casket, he smiled.

The rest of the night was spent preparing the casket to load. It proved to be a grueling undertaking, but around 1:30 a.m., it was all loaded and ready for the five-hour drive to St. Louis.

Sonya was bothered.

First, there was the concert in Chicago. It was very well attended and the reviews on social media were mostly positive. The only blemish, though, was the news of a missing twenty-two-year-old woman who was in attendance. She was separated from her friends, and they couldn't reach her. The hunt for the missing woman was in full force, but at the moment, there were no leads. Sonya was worried and hated the thought of someone getting hurt at one of their shows. And on top of this, she was confused about the new member of their crew.

"So, you just hired this stranger to be your drum tech?" Sonya asked Matt, as they sat together on the long bus ride to St. Louis. "What about Phil?"

"No, Thurston hired him, because I guess Phil just took off," Matt replied and looked out of the window. "I texted him, and all he would say was that he needed a change. Now he's ghosting me." He shook his head. "It's weird. But on the plus side, the new guy did a great job and was much faster than Phil. Unbelievably fast, really."

"Do you even know his name?" she asked.

"I think Thurston said his name was Danny and that he was going to meet us at The Fabulous Fox in St. Louis."

Sonya sat back in her seat and thought about the mysterious guy who first appeared in her hallway, then at the show, and now was their drum tech. She wondered if she should tell Wolf about the encounter, but decided against it, for now. After all, Danny intrigued her, and she didn't want him fired before she could find out more about him.

Sonya closed her eyes, and her thoughts returned to the missing woman. She hoped that she would be found soon.

Soon, the motion and white noise of the bus put her to sleep.

She slept as the bus continued south along I-55 until suddenly her eyes opened, startled by a voice in her head. She looked out of the window to see a white hearse move slowly forward. Its only markings were the letters A, U, and E on the window; the rest was scratched off. *Probably the name of the funeral home that used to own it.* Now it belongs to who? she wondered.

The name Danny popped into her head along with a calm voice that said, "See you soon, Sonya."

She whispered his name, "Danny?" and watched as the hearse drove ahead out of sight.

Danny had Robert rent a small condo with a garage, the idea being that the hearse could stay in the garage, the casket could stay in the hearse, and Danny could stay in the casket. This job would call for a lot of moving around, and the casket was too cumbersome to keep moving in and out of hotel rooms. I would be a perfect solution and would allow Danny, when not helping set up for the gigs, to prowl many new places and to take care of his needs.

The first show in St. Louis was approaching, and he only planned on turning up and doing his part. He was more eager than ever to get to know Sonya.

As darkness hit on the day of the St. Louis gig setup, Danny exited the garage and flew in bat form to The Fabulous Fox. It was impressive and reminded him of the gothic concert halls from home.

The stage and most of the sound system were already in place when he fluttered in from the back curtain. There was a lot of commotion, and no one even looked his way as he changed back to his human form.

At the back of the stage were the large cases that he assumed were the drums. Having left in such a hurry the other night, he had not helped take everything down and therefore wasn't sure how it all went back together. He did his best to recall the order of things as he unloaded the bags and attempted to assemble it all from memory. He did have a superlative memory, and it seemed to look the same. Next, he found microphones and attached them to the stands and clipped some of them to the individual drum rims. Again, everything looked correct. There was a bag with sticks and other odd-looking mallets inside that he remembered hanging on the drum to the right side of Matt.

On the drumheads themselves, he recalled seeing small green circles, which were not there. He found them inside the bag with the sticks and applied them in various spots, not really knowing what they were for. He moved the seat into position and took out a stick and hit the first drum on the left. It sounded good. He had a good ear and found that by moving the small green circles around, he could make different sounds. He moved them until they sounded like he knew drums should sound.

"What the hell?"

Danny looked up to see a heavyset man looking down at the drums and shaking his head.

"Hey, buddy, do you even know what you are doing?" The man didn't wait for an answer but went to work changing things around and in no time had things shifted, the way he wanted them.

Danny watched him carefully and took a mental note of the whole process. Next time, he would know exactly what to do.

The man walked over to Danny. "Look, man, I know you are new, but if you're not sure about something, just ask me. Around here, I'll be your best friend. My name's Hank." He extended his hand. "Man, your hands are cold—and I thought my hands were cold. Better go and warm up those fingers."

"Thanks," Danny said, thinking that Hank's hand felt cold too.

"Just poor circulation. Thank you for the help. I'll get the setup correct next time."

"I know you will, and you should stick around for the whole take down this time. Everyone helps until it's all finished—you just took off after your part. That's not how it works. There were a few guys not happy with having to do your job as well as their own."

Danny smiled and said, "Sorry, I had a previous commitment that night. It won't happen again."

"I know," said Hank. "Welcome aboard."

"Thank you," Danny said and went back to tuning up the drumheads. *Maybe I should learn how to play these things myself,* he thought. After all, he had seen more guys play the drums over the last hundreds of years than most.

When the drums were all tuned to his liking, he decided to give it a try.

Danny lifted his drumsticks and started in slowly. Then he built the beat, eventually into a rhythm unlike anything he had heard. It surprised him how easy it was. It was a kind of style that was a combination of various beats all put together—and it was working. He was even amazing himself. When he stopped, he looked down at the sticks, mesmerized. Then the clapping started.

Danny looked up to all the stagehands standing on the stage and some looking down from the riggings. They were all putting their hands together. He also heard comments like "cool man," and "where did you learn that?"

Then he saw her. She was in the crowd, clapping with the rest and smiling. She walked over.

Danny put the sticks back into the bag and stood up. "That was amazing," Sonya said. "What band are you in?"

"I'm not," he answered. "In fact, that was my first time. I thought I'd just sit down and give it a go. I'm just a drum tech."

"Yeah, right, I was standing next to Hank while you were giving it a go, and he said you are a much better drummer than you are a tech. Come on, what's your story? I'm sure there's more to you than scaring defenseless girls in hotel hallways." Sonya paused, looking for any kind of reaction to that comment. She got none. "Anyway, I know it was you, but I wasn't afraid. In fact, if you hadn't just disappeared, I might have invited you into my room." She smiled and turned to walk away.

"I wanted to meet you," he said.

"Meet me after the gig—after you are finished with the load up," she said and left the stage.

Soon, the concert was in full swing. For a while, Danny just watched the stage and watched Sonya. She was, after all, the reason she was here. As he took in Sonya dancing sultrily around the stage with her guitar, it occurred to him that she was not the goddess that he had first pursued. She was only another very talented guitar player. Still, he was anxious to get to know her better, and his thoughts toggled between the upcoming date and taking care of Matt's drums.

There wasn't much to do as the band played, and he didn't feel the need to watch Sonya the entire time. So he decided to take a walk and mingle with the crowd.

That night, after the gig, Danny and Sonya went for a walk in a park that was a few blocks away from The Fabulous Fox. The conversation was mostly about music—likes and dislikes.

They had the park to themselves except for a few late-night prowlers, mostly stray cats and dogs. Sounds from the city were always present: sirens in the distance, cars revving their engines, and wind rustling the leaves in the trees.

Perhaps because of his lack of companionship through the centuries, and especially in recent decades, Danny found talking to Sonya was a struggle, and when the so-called date was approaching an end, he was almost relieved. *How strange to want something so much and then be somewhat ready to let it go.* He couldn't tell if Sonya was feeling the same way. Still, the walk was not a complete disaster, ending with a short kiss and hug during which Danny could smell Sonya's blood through her soft skin and resisted the urge to satisfy his needs. *She's definitely not a vampire*, he thought.

"Your lips are frigid," she said and pulled back from the hug.

"It's the cold night air." Danny smiled and said, "I'm from a much warmer climate."

"Warmer than Missouri? Maybe the equator."

"I think I feel so cold because you are so hot," Danny said, amused at his own wit, and went in for another hug, and this time she endured his frigid touch a little longer and then pushed him away.

"I'm starved," she said and ran off. "I'll race you to the all-night café." When she got to the door of the café, Danny was already standing by the door.

"Impressive," Sonya said when they sat down at a booth. "I think you are keeping a secret from me."

"Everyone has their secrets." The conversation during the meal was mostly about the band and the upcoming shows. When Denny realized the time, he set down enough cash to pay, excused himself, and ran out of the café.

"Rude," Sonya said softly, then finished her coffee and walked back to the hotel alone.

She went up to Wolf's room first. She knew he'd be awake, and she wanted to ask him about his impression of Danny and share about his strange actions during their so-called date.

"I know he's not telling me everything," Sonya said. "He's not lying to me, just not telling me everything—quite the expert in avoidance."

Wolf just shook his head and said, "I've been wondering about him as well. You're correct, he's not who he seems, but I've got an idea."

"What?" asked Sonya.

"That, my dear, is a conversation for another time. Right now, we both need to get some sleep." He escorted her to the door. "For now, try not to get *too* close with our new drum tech." She smiled, said she wouldn't, and left for her own room.

Setting up the drum kit and tuning heads to perfection was now second nature to Danny. He was so fast and efficient that he also took over running the mics and setting the volumes on the mixer.

One thing that the other stagehands looked forward to was Danny's drum solo after the drum kit was put into place. It seemed to get more and more complex each time.

Matt was so impressed that he started to let Danny play a couple of songs during each show. His solo was always a crowd pleaser. It was Wolf's idea mostly because he was observing from the shadows the unusual pace at which Danny was becoming a tier one drummer, and it was not normal for a human to do this.

Every three to four days presented another city and another show, and all the while, the relationship between Danny and Sonya grew in small amounts. Neither wanted to frighten the other away, and neither felt an intense passion for the other. But as they spent more time together, they became more and more comfortable together. To Danny, the companionship was a refreshing change.

After a show in Colorado Springs, both Sonya and Danny were invited to Wolf's room for cocktails and conversation. "You two seem to be hitting it off quite well," said Wolf as he dropped a large round ice cube into his glass. "Anything you want to tell me?"

Sonya looked at Danny for help with an answer. He shrugged his shoulders. "We enjoy each other's company, but we won't let anything get in the way of our jobs."

"I'm sure not," Wolf said, then looked to Sonya. "I measure people by their production, and as of now, Sonya, you're at the top of your game, and there isn't one better lead guitarist in the industry—or prettier one, I might add." Then he turned to Danny. "And you are becoming quite the drummer. Very impressive and without any lessons."

Danny didn't answer—he had no answer.

Danny and Sonya were mostly quiet during the rest of the visit, with Wolf talking about his past, name-dropping at every opportunity. Finally, Sonya got up and said, "I need some rest. We'll see you at breakfast." She grabbed Danny by the hand. "See me to my room, Danny?"

"It'll be my pleasure," Danny said as he was escorted from the room. They said their goodbyes to Wolf, leaving him to think, and went down the hall together.

At the door to her room, Sonya asked, "Well, do you want to come in?"

"Absolutely," Danny said. An invitation was all he needed. "But just for a bit."

They sat together on the small love seat beside the bed. Danny no longer felt the strong draw toward her that had brought him to join the stage crew. He did like her and didn't want to hurt her, and he was getting the message that she felt the same about him.

They talked, shared lots of laughs, and some hand-holding, but no more. After an hour or so, they gave each other the usual hug—no kiss this time—and Danny left. And on the bat-flight back to the VRBO, Danny's mind was not on Sonya, but on the exhilarating feeling that sitting behind a set of drums and performing gave him. He was becoming addicted to this feeling.

Over the course of three months, they had played close to twenty shows. All were well received. But The Wolf Mixon Band had one dark curtain hanging over the tour. At a dozen gigs, there was some-one, usually female, who disappeared—and those missing were never found.

Security was beefed up, but that didn't help.

The audiences were getting smaller.

Eventually, the press surrounding the missing fans became so intense that Wolf and the rest of the band members decided to end the tour, after one last show.

The last show was in Phoenix, Arizona.

Matt sounded great during the show as usual. When Matt sounded good, the whole band sounded good.

There were no issues during the performance, which allowed Danny to sneak off and intermingle with the crowd. He always returned before the show was over, and no one seemed to be the wiser. Then, when the show was over, he carefully put everything back the way he had found it at setup.

That's what he'd done this night too; now he only had to finish packing all the equipment into the truck. After the last piece was loaded, he turned to find Sonya standing in the entryway and obviously distressed. "Someone is missing again," she said.

"That's horrible," Danny said slowly. "Hopefully, he just went home with someone else?"

"He was with a group; they came on a bus. They said this man would never have gone with anyone else." Sonya glared at him. "How did you know the missing person was a man?"

Danny said nothing and walked toward her. In the glow of the sodium streetlights of the loading dock, his eyes appeared to have a reddish glow. Her eyes dropped to his tie, and suddenly, she backed away.

"Is that blood? Danny, do you have anything to do with the missing people?" Her eyes became fearful, as if she was starting to connect the dots. That he knew this missing person was a man. That there was red on his tie. And that all disappearances had started at the concert in Chicago, where he joined the band. "I think you should stay away from me," she said.

Danny had made a promise to himself not to use his mental powers on her, but didn't hesitate in this circumstance. He continued to glare into her eyes, bared his teeth, and said, "Don't be afraid, Sonya. I had nothing to do with this."

"Yes, you did. I can tell you are lying. I know when people are lying."

She held up her hand, and a large instrument crate, that was sitting on the dock next to the truck, flew at Danny. He put up his hand in defense to block the impact.

She had not been affected by his hypnotism. "Are you a vampire?" he asked as he threw the crate back to the dock.

"A what?" she answered. "A vampire? No! They don't exist. Are you mental?"

"No, I just wanted to meet you. Now I'm not so sure." Danny watched as she turned and ran back inside, calling for help. He contemplated running back to the condo, but instead, he went inside after her.

Inside the hall was dark, and in the middle of the stage stood Sonya. She was surrounded by the rest of the band.

Danny stopped about ten feet from the group.

Wolf stepped forward and said, "I've had my suspicions about you for a while, in part because of how skilled you have become at playing the drums in such a short time. A skill that takes most percussionists years to perfect." Wolf paused and smiled. "Normally, having a vampire join the group would have been fine, but when they feed from the patrons and cause the whole tour to come to a screeching halt, then I need to step in. I, too, see the blood on your tie. Matt, would you go over and inspect that stain for me?"

Matt walked over to Danny, dropped his head down, and smelled. He then stood up and, with a snarling smile, displayed his own fangs to Danny. "Yes, this is blood, and a good vintage, I should add."

"Thank you, Matt. You can step back now." Wolf approached Danny and said in a low voice. "You see, Danny, I have nothing against vampires. I have some in my band. That makes eight, counting me and a few of our stagehands." From behind the group, six figures stepped out of the shadows. One Danny recognized—it was Hank. "The other two have their own unique identities." Wolf looked over at Sonya, who was staring at him with disbelief. "Sorry, dear, I had always meant to tell you, but sometimes it's better to be discreet."

"You're all vampires?" she asked and stepped back.

"No, not all of us," Wolf continued. "Reed here hails from a different breed—he's a werewolf and is the reason we don't schedule our gigs on the nights of the full moon. I always thought Reed should have my name—a wolf named Wolf." This caused a few laughs from the others.

"My deepest apologies, my dear Sonya. Don't be afraid—you are one of us, just with a different kind of power." Wolf turned back toward Danny. "You see, Sonya isn't afraid of you, she is afraid of destroying you—she has had the power to do just that all along. Therefore, she must like you a little."

Danny backed away. "I could still fit in—I just didn't know the rules."

"They're common-sense rules, Danny," Wolf snarled. "You should've known not to dirty the water in your own pool, and now, unfortunately, you must pay for ruining our tour." He bared his fangs and hissed. The others joined in and swarmed around Danny as he turned into a bat and flew up in a desperate escape. It was Hank who jumped up and grabbed him.

"Put him in a cage," Wolf roared.

Reed brought over a small black cage that was one of the props from the show. He removed the plastic raven and shoved the frantic bat inside, shut the door, and secured the latch. Danny, in bat form, went ballistic, hitting one side of the cage, then the other, trying to regain his freedom. Eventually, he gave up the fight and rested at the bottom of the cage, badly wounded and breathing heavily.

Wolf looked over at Sonya, who was staring down, trying to process the insanity of the situation. She had a look that was a mixture of confusion, disbelief, and betrayal. Wolf put his hand on her shoulder. "Again, forgive me."

She looked into his eyes, gave a hint of a smile, and nodded two times. Wolf also smiled and gave her a hug. After a few seconds, he pulled back but kept both hands on the top of her shoulders and spoke. "I want you to take the cage and do with it what you feel is right." She tried to protest but was silenced when Wolf placed an index finger to her lips. "It's going to be fine, I promise," he whispered. And he turned and walked away.

The rest of the band and crew moved away from the cage and proceeded to disappear in various directions. When they were all gone, Sonya walked over and knelt down. "Apparently, everyone had secrets." She picked up the cage and carried it out of the backstage door.

Danny woke in a dark alley—the exact location was unclear. His face was wet, which was strange because it wasn't raining. Realizing that the sun was about to rise, he looked around and saw a dumpster near the back of the alley. He climbed in and lowered the lid. *This will have to do,* he thought. At least until nightfall, when he could get his bearings and find his way back to his casket in the hearse.

Before he fell asleep, he recalled the events that had led him to this predicament. Then he looked down at his tie and found the bloodstain that had betrayed him. He removed the tie and threw it aside. *How careless of me.*

Danny realized that his time with this band and Sonya was over. However, she had let him go free, and that was a positive note. He smiled. Maybe one day they could reconnect. Until then, he would miss her, but the part he would miss the most would be playing the drums. He had become quite good, and when Matt allowed him to play at the shows, the thrill was like no other. "I'll do that again," he whispered to himself as his body shut down into a state somewhere between sleep and death.

The Wolf Mixon Band established a European tour a few months later. Matt had convinced Phil to rejoin as his drum tech, and to the relief of the concertgoers, no one else turned up missing during the shows.

Sonya remained as the lead guitarist, accepting the others for who they were. She hadn't given Danny much thought since she pulled him out of the cage and laid him on the cold cement of a dark alley. At the time, she had wondered if he would wake before the sun came up, and not wanting to take the chance of killing him in this fashion, she had poured water on him from a discarded bottle and disappeared as he opened his eyes.

One day, when she was lying on the hotel couch, enjoying a cocktail with Wolf and thumbing through her guitar magazine, she came across an article giving rave reviews for a drummer who had recently joined the Broken Mirror band. The band's former drummer had mysteriously left the month before, citing that he needed a change.

Change my ass, she thought as she looked at the picture from the article—it was Danny, clear as day, staring back at her. "Hey, Wolf, have you ever heard of a band called the Broken Mirror?"

"Oh sure, they are out of Australia. Cohen Downs, the leader, and I spent some time haunting London in our early vampire years. I think it was the music scene that tore us apart. Why?"

"Another vampire band—imagine that. Well, apparently, they have a new drummer." She held the magazine up for Wolf to see.

Wolf smiled. "Well, good for Danny. Let us hope he has learned from his mistakes—for I feel it won't end as well with Cohen."

"Let us hope," Sonya said and turned the page.

Danny had been able to acquire his new position as drummer with Broken Mirror in much the same way he found his drum tech position in Wolf's band. However, Cohen, the bandleader and also a vampire, welcomed him with open arms.

As it turned out, Cohen was well aware of Danny's misfortune with his previous engagement and made it clear to Danny that one strike with him and he was out, never to play again—anywhere. Danny had learned his lesson, and feasting from the concertgoers would not even be possible anymore, not with him sitting behind the drum kit during the entire show and no longer mingling with the human appetizers that came to watch.

He often thought of Sonya and had read in a music journal that The Wolf Mixon Band and Broken Mirror were booked into the same all-day concert in Vegas the following summer. *That should be interesting*, he thought with a smile. But first, Broken Mirror had more shows on their own.

That night was the opening night of a two-day, sold-out concert in Boston. The opening band, The Assassin Trolls, did their best to warm up the eager crowd.

When it came time for Broken Mirror to take the stage, Danny had eased himself onto the drum throne and started the heavy beat of one of Broken Mirror's signature songs. The crowd went wild.

The rest of the band raced on stage, grabbed their instruments and joined in, softly at first, then building up to a deafening thunder. Last to the stage was Cohen Downs. The audience became louder than before and began shouting his name in unison. Danny Barrow was in heaven—as much as a vampire can be in heaven, that is.

Death by Mangrove

THE FLORIDA KEYS are a great place for vacationing, friendly people, great fishing, blue waters, fantastic restaurants—but then there are the mangroves.

The word mangrove was new to me the first time that I visited the Keys. Now, I feel like an expert, but I will get to that later. My girlfriend and I had been wanting to get away from the grind of working life to visit what they call paradise. We landed in a super nice resort in Key Largo, which is mentioned in the song "Kokomo" by the Beach Boys. "Why not just go to Kokomo?" I asked her, but as it turns out, there's no place in the Florida Keys with this name—apparently, the Beach Boys made it up. I'm pretty sure we weren't the only ones to set off for this imaginary paradise. Disappointment aside, there are lots of other paradises to choose from—Key Largo was our choice for our first trip.

Our hotel was on the Gulf side of the Keys and promised to have great swimming, fishing options, an amazing restaurant, and, of course, a spa for relaxing massages. To get there, we booked a flight into the Miami International Airport, and from there, we would rent a car and drive to Key Largo—simple enough.

The stay in Key Largo was relaxing and exciting. We booked a private fishing trip for the day. Our guide's name was Ozzy—short for Osbaldo. He had lived in the Keys for twenty years, moving there while in grade school. His boat had a large flat deck on the front where my girlfriend and I would stand and cast out the lures and bait that Ozzy provided. "Cast close to the Mangrove," he would say, and almost every time, we would hook a fish and sometimes get them to the boat.

Some of the fish we kept; some we released. He seemed to know the difference between a keeper and "you can't eat this one."

One time, a shark about six feet long snatched the fish right off my hook. "Tiger shark—don't fall in the water," Ozzy said, with the tone of everyday nonsense. It would have been nice to know that fact ahead of time.

We continued to weave in and out of the passageway with mangroves on both sides. "These mangrove plants sure grow thick on these islands," I said.

"Actually, the mangroves were here first. They have a root system that allows them to grow and to be sturdy on the bottom of shallow waters. Their roots spread out like a tripod. Then, the sand is trapped in the root systems, and the islands are formed. The roots also provide a protective shelter for all kinds of fish and wildlife." Then he lowered his voice. "You never know what you'll find under the mangrove." This comment led to a sudden chill down my spine as I thought of alligators and snakes and all the things you want to avoid.

At the end of the day, we ended up keeping around ten fish. Ozzy cleaned them with a hose and bucket, filleted them with a knife, and handed them to us in a plastic sack. "Take these to the resort restaurant, and they'll cook them for your dinner tonight." We thanked him, paid him, and headed to the restaurant to drop off our catch. It led to the best dinner we had on our visit.

The massages were relaxing; the food was to die for; and the sunsets were breathtaking—then it was time to go home. Sitting by the dock on the morning of our departure, I heard a strange whisper coming from the mangrove next to the water. "Kokomo," I thought the voice said. I listened for more, but there was nothing but silence. My mind was playing tricks—I was just thinking about that song.

The flight home was uneventful, but it was kind of sad to be leaving paradise to go back to the drudgery of day-to-day life. My girlfriend—her name is Kara, by the way—was just as sad. We promised to visit paradise as often as we could—hopefully every year.

Time can get away so fast. We didn't get back to the Florida Keys for twelve years, and during that time, Kara became my wife.

Work-life balance is something we all need to be aware of in order to minimize the ups and downs of stress that life delivers. There was a kind of panic when Kara and I realized that our jobs were our lives and time was beginning to speed up. Still without kids, unless you consider Gustavo, our mini-Labradoodle, and nicknamed Gus, our child—he certainly was.

So, years later, it was a weekend in November. The daily temperatures were making the mercury in the thermometer go in the wrong direction as well as making my weekend backyard barbecue routine less than pleasant. Even Gus was at the back door asking to go inside rather than sniffing for bugs in the garden. *At least my reliable smoker was not abandoning me*, I thought to myself as I applied the last coating of sauce to the baby backs.

As Kara opened the door to rescue Gus from the cold, she asked me, "How much longer, hun?"

"Twenty minutes tops."

Kara closed the door, and I closed the lid to the smoker. I headed inside to get a beer. Passing the flower bed beside the door, I noticed a strange plant growing up between the dead petunias that I'd been meaning to discard. It was basically a long stem with about a half dozen green leaves at the top pointing to the sky. The plant looked foreign yet oddly familiar—and how was it growing in this cold environment? Bending down to get a better look, the plant made noises, and they sounded like words. "Come back to Gus," it kind of sounded like, but I wasn't exactly sure that was what it said because it was barely audible. And why would a plant be talking about my dog? *Maybe it was "come back to us,"* I thought, which gave me more of a shiver, and this one was not caused by the cold afternoon. Besides, plants can't talk, but I think the wind can sound like talking when it blows through the leaves.

I left the plant and went inside. "Kara, you need to come outside and look at this plant in the garden."

"Kevin, the plants are dead."

"Not this one, believe it or not, I thought it was calling to our dog." She gave me a slight eye roll and led me outside to look.

The plant was gone. Not just "something pulled it out" gone, but "never been there" gone. "It was just here—I swear."

"No more beer for you today, honeybunny." She stepped back inside and added, "Hurry with the ribs, I'm hungry."

I continued to stare at the spot where the plant had vanished for a moment, then went inside thinking, *Now I need that beer more than ever.*

When funny and unexplainable things happen in your life, it's sometimes easier to forget them and move on. However, this unexplainable voice coming from the plant in the garden that was never there was bothersome—and why did the plant appear to be familiar? I recalled that similar situation a long time ago, in the resort at Key Largo. *Funny, I hadn't thought of that for years. What had the plant said then? It was something about the song Kokomo,* I thought. And did the disappearing plant look like a mangrove? I really had no idea. Who can remember exactly what things looked like that long ago?

The smoked rib dinner was phenomenal. Gus begged me to give him a bone. I never do, but he always asks. The dishes were minimal, mostly dishwasher things.

"Maybe we need to take a long overdue vacation," I said to the sink as Kara walked behind me.

"That would be nice," she said. "Maybe a cruise—I hear they're very relaxing. Not sure what we would do with Gus."

Pets, as much joy as they add to your life, do also present problems when it comes to travel. This is where family members who owe you favors come in handy.

"My brother, Jonathan, will watch him. You know how much he loves dogs." Actually, if Jonathan loved dogs, he would probably own one, but since I am constantly helping him with his numerous summer projects, how could he turn me down? "I was thinking of visiting the Florida Keys—reliving the trip we took before we were married." When no response was given, I looked back to find myself alone in the kitchen. "Hun, where are you?"

I went into the living room and saw her vanish up the stairs, calling back to me as she went, "Great idea! I'll start packing immediately."

Apparently, a vacation was way overdue.

Packing for a business trip is tedious; packing for fun in the sun in the Keys is invigorating. Mostly, you need shorts, flip-flops, and cool flowery shirts—why be a tourist if you can't look like one? With the internet as our tour guide and working with a substantially larger budget, I was able to plan for a more-than-luxurious vacation. We weren't going to Key Largo this time. This time, we were going to stay in a more upper-scale location near Marathon—a place called Key Colony Beach, where if you could afford it, you could rent a beautiful house with a boat dock in case you wanted to rent a boat or maybe just kayaks, and best of all came with a private pool. Yes, I went all out, even first-class plane tickets to Key West, and why not. I mean, the mangroves were calling my name.

It was obvious to me that Gus was super excited to stay at Jonathan's by his running around the living room, jumping on furniture, and knocking over the plant stand under the window. Jonathan, however, did not appear as excited. "We'll be back before you know it, Bro."

Jonathan was staring at the five-page handwritten instructions with a horrified look on his face. Then he looked down at Gus, who was sitting like a championship show dog in front of him. Jonathan knelt, and Gus gave him his paw. "Well, I think we'll manage somehow."

Kara and I stayed long enough to where we felt that Jonathan had an adequate grasp on the dog directions, then said our good-byes to the two of them and drove off to the house to finish packing. Flying first class allowed us to take two large suitcases as well as two carry-on bags. Probably more than we needed for our two-week stay in Marathon but it also gave us room to bring home souvenirs.

Flying can be fun or tedious, depending on the day. Fortunately, we survived a short two-hour delay in Atlanta by relaxing in a wine bar and answering a few text messages from Jonathan about Gus and his newly acquired stomach problems. "He must be a little nervous in his new environment," Kara said, then added, "Poor Gus."

"Poor Gus, you mean, poor Jonathan." Dog stomach problems are the worst. We promised to check back with him when we got to Key West. This was going to cost us a nice souvenir.

The pilots were able to make up some of the lost time in the air, allowing for plenty of time to get our rental and head to Key Colony while the sun was shining. I had chosen a small Ford SUV from the Avis lot, connected my phone to the Apple CarPlay, and set the GPS to our house on the beach. The drive was beautiful with the Atlantic on one side and the Gulf on the other. The color of the water is stunning and exactly what you would expect paradise water to look like. For an early dinner, we stopped at a thatched-covered restaurant next to the road where we drank piña coladas and split a tender grouper sandwich. Paradise food and drink was also living up to their billing.

"Thank you for bringing me back to the Keys," Kara said to me when we got back into the car. "While I'm at work, sometimes, I find myself thinking about that first trip we took down here."

"Of course," I answered and smiled.

"They say that you can never relive the special times in your life, but I'm going to do my best. So far, it's everything I remember, and I'm not going to let anything spoil this for us." She reached over and grabbed my hand. "Key Colony sounds beautiful."

"Outside of the Beach Boys' made-up town of Kokomo, it was the best place I could find." Without looking, I could tell her smile grew even wider. "Besides, the name Key Colony wouldn't rhyme with go." Now she was laughing.

The sun was setting behind us, though we still had an hour and fifteen minutes before we would turn right into Key Colony, so I decided to turn on the radio. I found a country station playing our favorite Chris Stapleton song. We sang along with Chris and then with Shaboozey after that. I glanced down at the dashboard screen.

"That's odd," I said.

"What is it, dear?"

"The last time I checked, the GPS said we would turn right, and now it says we'll be turning left." I found a place to turn off to check my phone. "I'll just reset it." I ended the route and typed in the address of the VRBO. The maps app now showed we had fifty minutes until a right turn. "That's better," I said. "I must have bumped my phone when messing with the radio."

It was now dusk. After checking for other cars, I pulled out onto the road with the radio belting out more current country songs. It was a beautiful night, and in my mind, I was imagining floating in the pool and drinking Mai Tai's with Kara.

"What happened to our country music?" Kara said.

Coming back to reality, I heard the radio playing a familiar song by the Beach Boys. Then it hit me. Kokomo. The radio was playing "Kokomo"—the song we were joking about earlier and not a country song. "That's a little creepy," I said and reached down to change the channel.

"Don't change it," Kara said with her pouty face. "I like this song."

"Me too, but for some reason, it's giving me the creeps." I pulled my hand back and let the song play. After the song ended, the station was back to playing country again. *So weird*, I thought.

The sky was now dark with a partial moon illuminating the water and the many boats racing into their harbors. The GPS was still set to turn right—we had forty-one minutes before the turn. Up ahead, an old sign caught my eye. Mostly because it looked like it could blow over at any minute. The painted letters were faded and hard to read. As we approached it, I could see that it read: "WELCOME TO KOKOMO" and in smaller print read: "NEXT LEFT."

"What the hell," I said, making Kara look up from her phone. "Do you see that?"

"I do," she said. "And look at the screen." The GPS screen was now telling me to make a left turn in a quarter of a mile. "What's going on, Kevin? I thought you told me Kokomo didn't exist."

"That's what I read, but obviously, someone thought it funny to put up a sign. Probably to get people to turn and the roads leads to some crappy gift store or something." I pressed down hard on the accelerator. "Well, I'm not turning."

I turned my head to look down the road that claimed to be Kokomo. It was dark, with overgrown trees growing tall on both sides and touching at the top, creating a creepy dark cave. My foot came off the accelerator and slammed on the break. The car skidded to a stop—good thing there wasn't a car behind us.

"What are you doing, Kevin?" Kara had both hands on the dashboard and her hair was thrown forward, covering her eyes. "Are you crazy!"

"I'm just curious," I said and turned the car down the dark road. Thinking back, I'm not sure why I turned. It was like my mind and my body were on different pages. After all, I was anxious to get to Key Colony, and a detour was not helping. Regardless, I drove the car down the gloomy road to . . . to where? Kokomo?

The road went on for much longer than I could imagine. *Are the Keys really this wide?* I thought. The whole time Kara was begging me to turn around—but something was pulling at me that was stronger than her voice. I didn't want to ignore her pleas but couldn't resist the force that was guiding me. Guiding me to where? I had no idea.

Then, the narrow road opened up into a small sunny community center, and there were people walking around talking and laughing. At this hour, it wasn't possible for the sun to be shining. But it was.

I pulled the car over, shut off the car, opened the door, and got out. "Are you coming?" I asked Kara. She had her head down and was crying. "Suit yourself." I slammed the door shut.

A couple who was dressed for the beach walked past me. "Hi, where are we?" I asked. They just ignored me and kept walking like I wasn't even there. *Rude,* I thought and looked back to the car. The sun vanished. The car was parked by a path that led down to a rocky beach. The path to the beach was lined with dark and dense vegetation. *Are those the mangroves?* I thought. The wind came up and blew through the leaves. "Want to defy a little bit of gravity?" whispered the wind.

"No!" I yelled and got back into the car. Kara still had her head down and then looked up when I slammed the door.

"What are you doing?" She was hysterical.

"We've gotta get out of here," I said as I started the car and smashed down on the gas. The car turned wildly around, narrowly missing going over into the mangroves. The tires caught and off we sped back down the road.

It didn't take us long to get back to the main road. My heart was racing, and when I looked back down at the GPS, it now said to turn left in thirty-nine minutes, and country music was back on the radio. *I need a drink*, I thought. "Me too," Kara said. I must have said it out loud.

When you do something stupid like I had done by turning down an unknown road for no reason, you would expect a lecture from your wife. She said nothing. I thought it strange, but not wanting a lecture, I didn't question the silence.

We arrived at our bungalow in paradise with no further incidents. The house was even better than the pictures on the listing, except for the pool being slightly smaller than we thought. No problem there being just the two of us—at least it was warm. The bed was comfortable, and as I fell asleep, I tried to recall the strange detour I had taken, but the details were fading like dreams do.

The next morning, while I was enjoying my first cup of coffee for the day, I walked down past the pool to the steps that led to the canal. As I approached the steps, I hesitated. On both sides were thick growths of mangrove plants. They were so thick that you couldn't see through to the water and made a great privacy fence for the pool area. Grabbing the top of one of the branches, I examined the leaves. It seemed to be the same kind of leaf that mysteriously disappeared outside of my backyard. Although, I couldn't quite remember. I probably should have taken a picture of the plant growing in my backyard at home, had it not disappeared.

I continued down to the edge of the dock to inspect fishing possibilities. There were fish in the water, but I didn't know what kind. At the far end was a fish cleaning station, which told me I might have a chance to catch something. There was also a ladder that went down into the water—not sure that would be a great idea, remembering the shark encounter we had on our first visit. Upon turning back toward the steps, I froze. The mangrove branches were now touching when before they were spaced out at least three feet across. A strong gust of wind suddenly sent waves through the mangrove leaves, making a rustling sound. And within it was a distinct whisper. The whisper said, "I wanna take you down . . ." *Down to what?* I thought. Oh my god, it was lyrics from that damn Kokomo song. "Down to Kokomo?" I screamed. I did not receive an answer. In a state of panic, I ran up the stairs. The branches grabbed at me, but my momentum carried me through. I didn't stop until I was at the back door. Kara, having heard me scream, was there at the door.

"What's the matter, I thought you fell in."

"It's the mangroves—they're after me," I said, trying to catch my breath.

"Come inside, Keven." She pulled me through the door, and I collapsed to the floor. "Nothing is after you," she said. "Tell me what happened." Kara was giving me that "I think you are going crazy" look.

"Look down at the steps with the branches going all the way

across. They weren't that way at first." We both looked back down. Now, the mangrove branches looked like fine manicured hedges. There was nothing growing past the step railings. "What. Kara, that's not the way they were."

"Right, like the disappearing plant at the house," she said. "This vacation was supposed to help you relax; not make you go mental. I'm taking you to bed. You're obviously exhausted from the trip."

"Okay, but I'm not going mental. Don't you remember the song, 'Kokomo,' coming on the radio on the way here and the strange sign, and me turning down that creepy road?" Kara just stared at me with zero indication that she knew what I was talking about. "You don't remember, do you?"

"Oh, honey, I'm trying to, but you're scaring me." She was crying while at the same time trying to pull it together. She put her arms on my shoulder and turned me to face her. "Kevin, I think you're just tired. Hopefully, you'll feel better after your nap." She led me down the hall to our bedroom.

I woke up startled and jumped out of bed. "Kara!" I yelled. There was no answer. I slipped into my slippers and ran out of the bedroom door. The hallway seemed longer than usual as I made my way to the back of the house, stopping at the kitchen for a glass of water and then continuing to the screened-in area that looked down to the canal. Kara was sitting by the pool wearing the skimpiest bikini I'd ever seen. One that I didn't recognize. I opened the screen door, walked over, and stood behind her. The air was cold, not ideal for sunbathing. The sky was clear but gray.

"I feel rested now. Thanks for making me sleep," I said and reached down to touch the back of her chair. She turned around, and she was beautiful, but she was not Kara.

"I'm sorry, Kevin. I didn't hear you."

"Who are you?" I asked, looking around the backyard. "And where's Kara? She put me to bed." I reached into my pocket for my cell; it was not there. Panic set in.

The woman smiled and said, "Don't be afraid, Kevin. Kara is fine. She went back home after your accident." She reached her hand out.

"Who are you? What have you done with Kara?" I asked again.

"I told you she went home," she said, making a pouty face like Kara would have.

"Then why didn't Kara take me with her? She would not have left me," I said. "And what accident are you talking about, and how do you know my name?" She started walking backward toward the canal. Her eyes never left mine. The pout was gone, and the smile returned. She was motioning me to follow, and I was unable to resist. She stepped over rocks as if she knew they were there without look-ing. "I don't want to follow you," I said, but my legs started moving in her direction.

"Listen, Kevin, no one was able to find you after the accident. Not even after dragging the canal. You are officially a missing person," she said as if this was a good thing. "Now, I'm here to take you home," she said and took a couple of steps toward me. "Please follow me, 'cause I'm taking you to where you want to go." She turned and now she was heading to the mangroves. The slope was steep, but her feet never slipped. She stepped down into the water below the branches of the mangroves. Her body seemed to be disappearing before my eyes, and still, I continued to follow.

Then, it all came back to me as in a dream. The first time Kara put me into bed, I didn't stay in bed. I remember her saying, "You'll feel better after a nap, honey." She pulled the covers up to my chin and said, "I'll wake you in a few hours, and we can have some supper." She turned and left the room.

I threw off the covers, jumped up, and ran out of the room. I passed her in the hallway and continued running toward the patio door, threw it open, and ran down the sidewalk. The mangroves were again touching from both sides of the steps, but this time, there was no space between them in which to pass. I sped up, thinking that if I ran fast enough, I could break through to the canal like when we played the Red Rover game as kids. All I could think about was getting there and not being sure if I would take it fast or slow. *I must be going mad*, I thought. I should have run the other way. As I hit the branches, my forward motion was immediately halted, and I was being pulled sideways into the mangroves. It was like being pulled into the clutches of a huge spider, down into her web to be tranquilized and then eaten alive. I tried to scream, but nothing came out.

As I disappeared into the dark unknown of the mangrove, I saw Kara coming out of the door. She was calling my name and looking around. "Kara, I'm here! Help!" She ran down the hill and pulled me up onto the gravel, and then led me back up to bed. This time, I stayed in bed and fell asleep.

I should have stayed awake because here I am now, following the mysterious lady into the darkness even though I didn't want to go—just like not wanting to turn down a dark road but being unable to resist.

When one imagines what could be down under the mangroves, it is in no way comparable to the reality of what is actually there.

People disappear all the time in the Florida Keys, and now I know what happens to them. It is quite a sight down under the mangroves: the trash, the dead animals, and, of course, the human remains and bones. The overall smell is indescribable and, when you get used to it, quite pleasant. There are lots of disturbing things to see down here under the water intertwined with the roots of the mangrove. It gives "bodies in the sand" a whole new meaning.

The woman grabbed my hand and pulled me upward. As we resurfaced from the mangroves, there were others walking in and out. The couple who earlier ignored me came over and gave me hugs. "We have waited a long time for you," the woman said and kissed me on the cheek. Everyone was beautiful. I looked down to see my clothes had changed. Now I was in a bright green and gold Tommy Bahama shirt and shorts. I was beautiful too. Others also came up to greet me—everything was going to be okay.

Again, the woman grasped my hand and pulled me back down into the mangrove, but this time, I wanted to go—it was comforting, and a song was playing; it is my new favorite song, and I get to hear it over and over. *I wish Kara could be here,* I thought. *Too bad she went home. Maybe she will rejoin me someday.*

As it turns out, there is a place called Kokomo down in the Florida Keys. I'm not sure it's where I wanted to be, but it is where I am now, and it's quite peaceful. And from the depths of the mangroves, I can still tell my stories. But really—who's listening? I'm sure that I will find someone. I think I already have.

Acknowledgments

THIS BOOK WOULD NOT EXIST without the insight, guidance, and encouragement of several remarkable individuals.

First, my heartfelt thanks to **Robin Bethel**, my writing coach and editor—thank you for your thoughtful feedback, encouragement, and the many ways you helped shape these stories into their best form. Your advice, sharp eye, and steady encouragement made all the difference.

Huge thank you to **Katya Fishman**, my book publishing consultant, for your steady direction and expertise in guiding me through the maze and keeping everything on track.

Thanks also to **Jennifer Bisbing**, my proofreader, for your careful eyes and attention to every little detail. You helped polish this book to a shine.

A big shout-out to **Zack Smithey** for the killer cover art. You nailed the vibe I was going for—thank you.

To **Whitney Thatcher at Studio W Portraits**—thank you for capturing such a great author photo. Your talent made me look way cooler than I am.

Thanks to **Bryan Canter**, my audiobook publishing consultant, for navigating the world of audio with clarity and precision.

Appreciation also goes to **Victoria Wolf** of **Wolf Design and Marketing** for the awesome layout and a cover that really pops—you nailed it.

And most of all, thank you to my wife, **Lisa Baue**, for your love, support, and constant belief in me. Your encouragement kept me going from page one to the finish line. This book is as much yours as it is mine.

With gratitude,
Monte

About the Author

MONTE CRABBS is a retired school librarian, coach, drummer, and lifelong storyteller whose imagination knows no bounds. After years spent guiding young readers through the worlds of literature, he now crafts his own—dark, strange, and unforgettable. His stories blend horror, fantasy, and the uncanny, drawing inspiration from the eerie silences of empty libraries, the thunder of live drums, and the wild beauty of the Colorado landscape he calls home.

Monte lives with his wife, Lisa Baue, on a small ranch in Colorado, where the mountains whisper stories and the nights spark inspiration, demonstrating that it's never too late to pursue new passions and that the intersections of different paths can lead to the most fulfilling adventures.

Monte is currently working on his second collection of short stories as well as his first novel.

If you would like to know when new works are released, please visit his website.

www.montecrabbs.com